J

# THE DREAM /
## THUNDER ROAD *stories*
*and dreams 1955-1965*
## FIELDING DAWSON

157

*1972*

BLACK SPARROW PRESS

*los angeles*

The cover collage is by Fielding Dawson.

Note: the poem on page 112 is from *ALL: the collected short poems 1923-1958* by Louis Zukofsky (W. W. Norton) and is used with the poet's kind permission.

Black Sparrow Press
P.O. Box 25603
Los Angeles, California
90025

Library of Congress Cataloging in Publication Data

Dawson, Fielding, 1930-
  The dream/thunder road.

  I. Title.
PZ4.D27235Dr  (PS3554.A948)      813'.5'4      72-6937
ISBN 0-87685-113-8
ISBN 0-87685-112-X (pbk.)

## INTRODUCTION & DEDICATION

THE PROCESS *by which a story or a dream unfolds, even regardless of what either means, must be the same: inner contacts form, and in the complicated effort of conscious articulation I, at least, don't quarrel with which is which, because a story is a dream is a story, even if it isn't, but by its own energy and force to contact, of that it demands to be told, and I, the medium, merely follow:* merely, *because what's going on in there, trying to get said, awes me, that while I sleep another life goes on as if wide awake, as if wide awake was (it is) spinning images and emotions clashing and sparkling it's so sharply clear it's as if* it's the reality, *and often, to wake is disappointing (leave the magic land), just as to wake can be a blessing: from nightmare shock, yet in either instance, to adjust is tough, or as tough, in dreams' tenacity, as to try to fall asleep to dream, to leave one to enter the other, no matter which you can't wish a dream, and you can't wish consciousness; but if you're a real dreamer, and I am a real dreamer, you, like me, can* demand *to dream (it's a risk what you'll get), just as you can demand consciousness—and chance what you'll come up with.*

*So, some of these demanded me, and I followed; some of them are story-stories, and some of the stories are dreams, and some of them are dreams written, and some are a mixture of both; in commitment to action it's hard to say which, but the* writing *then, here, is an effort to form the endless contacts within my self, and selfs, awake or asleep, and to articulate not only that form, but hopefully the process whereby the form rises into its own,* to continue continuity, *and (typical of me, you might say), for all this I'm truly grateful to Dr. Conrad Sommer, in Saint Louis, and Dr. Arthur Lefford, in New*

*York—with me, that is, in New York; and also to the editors who in the dark days of the fight to write these pages, stuck with me and published them: Andrew Crozier, Tom Raworth, Tom Clark, Donald Phelps, Gil Sorrentino, Hank Chapin, and Aram Saroyan, and as Thanksgiving 1971 approaches, many bountiful thanks to John Martin for publishing this book.*

FIELDING DAWSON
10/25/71 NEW YORK

# TABLE OF CONTENTS

# THE DREAM/THUNDER ROAD

*in the snowslide of a priori*
*in flow and stir*

—KITASONO

# THE DREAM

NATHAN wrote AION in the dust: basic training was over.

He walked along the main street toward the center of town. He passed the Nationwide market and heard someone say his name. Whisper it. A hoarse whisper.

The afternoon was sunny. The sky was clear.

The voice said his name, and with the same harsh whisper, "Hey, Mithras—"

\* \* \*

There is a man who lives next to me in this building, and he listens to his radio.

Not hour after hour continually through the day. He listens consistently in the morning and at night; he doesn't listen to much music; he seems to enjoy narration.

He listens to the news.

At five thirty in the evening a station has a fifteen minute newsbreak followed by a weather report and sports roundup, at five forty-five another station has a fifteen minute newscast and at six another station has their newscast and at six fifteen another station has a fifteen minute news analysis. And he listens each evening to the news of the day; an analysis by a man with a dramatic name and dramatic voice.

I can't hear what they analyse, or what the news is, muffled voices through the wall are all I hear, and his occasional footfall and the sound of his door opening and closing as he comes and goes, and his lonely sleeping sounds in the nights.

Dan

\* \* \*

I just looked out of my window. It's snowing. I live in a hotel on 8th Avenue near 14th Street.

I came back to the hotel and took a nap. I think I'll go out and catch a cab. People want cabs when it snows. Especially crippled people from the Federation. They're grateful. You can see them in the doorway, waiting, uncertain.

I never need to ask.

HEY TAXI

Wave your hands and jump. When he pulls over you open the door and tell him to wait, then run over to the doorway where she's already coming out on her crutches. Help her in.

Back to the curb and look around. Nobody in sight. I'll catch one anyway.

HEY TAXI

You have to chase them sometimes. Or run in front. Jump high and fast. Wave your arms. When they stop tell them—you're broke. Anything. They'll curse and drive away. Perfectly all right. Wait for another. I like busy corners. 14th Street and 8th Avenue is good because it's busy and close to home. I can see my window. When it's snowing it's best.

Listen. Some funny things happen. I'm a cab catcher. I like it in the snow. The streets are white and the air is fresh and night time snow falls quiet. People huddle in doorways and under awnings. I run out in the middle of traffic and wave my arms, jump and yell TAXI. Night is terrific. The headlights are bright in my face and they see me wanting them.

I'd like to catch a couple but it's too late. I'll go to bed and think about it. The yellow ones. Hear those dogs? That's Mr. Johnson down the hall. He has six dogs. He loves dogs. I have to go to work tomorrow. An agency got me the job. People have a hard time getting jobs. My mind is tired. When my mind gets tired I want to sleep. Sometimes I come home from work early. The boss knows. He's a fine man. You can trust him. I'll see him tomorrow for sure.

\* \* \*

She came in the kitchen with an album of photographs her mother had given her and told me to look at them. The dawn of 1919. They were snaps of her as a girl and from then on. I looked at them while she put Frank Sinatra on the player. She came back in the kitchen and asked me if I wanted a stick of gum.
"No," I said.
She laughed. Silly, she said.

At the end of the summer I was in the bar where I go and she came in with the guy she had been seeing. She glanced and sneered at me and they sat down at a table and ordered. It was warm out and the door was open. I was sitting in front of the beer taps looking out at the busy city street. I had a few more drinks and fell into thought. When they left, she stopped beside me on the way; he went outside. So: she told him she would.

"You're really a case," she said. "You're sick. You drink until you can't talk and the next day hide behind your hangovers. You know?"

She paused. She was chewing gum and breathing fast. Shooting Spearmint in my face. The blackline on her right eye was a little off.

"Whiskey is ruining your life," she said.

She shifted to the other foot. She squinted her right eye and looked at me and chewed hard. I couldn't contain the smile. Her right shoulder twitched; she walked away and stopped at the doorway, turned. Her silhouette pointed a finger at me.

"You're fucked up."

She pivoted, marched out into the sunshine and put her hand in the crook of his arm.

\* \* \*

It was dark and cool and lonely.

I had waited at the side of the road for them to come from the party; I was looking into the hole in the small dirt curb the bulldozers had thrown up. The miniature deer was in there, and the rat-shape was crouched in front of my feet by the opening; as the others came down the road the deer dashed out around my feet and across the road.

Later the miniature killer deer got the rat—before, I stood on the unfinished highway looking into the city-like sewer grating in the small dirt curb the bulldozers had thrown up, waiting for the rat to try and escape. The handsome killer deer crouched at my feet peering into the grating, and as my elders came down the road the rat made his break, skittering across the road into the grass, but the killer deer was there waiting, and as the rat screamed I saw the killer's eyes, like tiny triangles glinting as off a headlight beam, and the rat in the grass with his throat cut. Is—

"Is that place, is that the place for rent?" I asked. Everyone had come, and then gone home. I pointed to the rickety platform in the trees.

She nodded. How wise she looked! I was dismayed—I wanted to sculpt right away, but how could I climb that bent ladder? I leaned out the window to see how high the trees went, but I couldn't look directly up, the sun was blinding and the branches were lost the trees went into the sky which blueness and brilliance of sun blasted my eyes and hurt my head in color.

I withdrew into the room seeing stars.

"I'm sorry," I said. "I can't rent it. I could never get in up there."

\*　\*　\*

He stood in the front yard as the house slanted toward and above the trees to the sky and in treetops the first floor seemed a concave cube. He ran in his underpants to the gate to get the mail as the man and woman came across the field, and was looking down from a height they were a hundred yards away coming across the long sloping matted-down field and he ran back in the yard moving his buttocks to hide them from his mind he felt girlish as the man and woman came through the gate, they stood between trees looking at him and I blushed and used the tree in front of him, he I maneuvered it between level lines of vision using the one closest to them as leverage and the man's face changed, the woman got prettier, at first she seemed plain and a little pockmarked, tho pretty, but now her hair was fluffy and dirty blonde and I saw her dusky face—her lips parted and she ducked behind the tree, the man reached for her and glanced at me but I stood as a force between trees and the man seemed torn between going to her and bringing her to him, his face was public—young oval, and he wore a white shirt, slacks, and he was now ugly, his skin was dusty and he had darkly smoking eyes and for a moment he was plump, he held out his hand, I stood side by side with him and before the woman had gone behind the tree I had looked into her face, I didn't see it change (she was smiling), she beamed at me. Her husband looked at her and looked at me, her lips parted and for a moment she was the Marilyn taller thinner more shallow in face and she showed fear, a cinematic flavor swept over the lawn and the man held his hand above a wooden plate—three plates waist high or higher and he touched on like it was a pipestand and in his easy chair he put his pipe down and said, "Well, what are we going to drink? And when? And why not now?" I laughed gleefully—"We'll go up to my place." I jerked my thumb towards the platform inside the old building and they stood close together with a bottle of vodka in my mind. The field dipped and slanted to my right and a little in front of me; to my left the house and the lawn seemed full of sticks and twigs and large trees; I was a little confused; who would go? The man laughed; she had one hand on his shoulder the other lightly on his elbow yet she seemed apart from him while tending towards him, our—my eyes concentrated on the to-bacco in the walnut saucer pipestand, it came from his fingers and looked, I looked at it like it was money; the man did too;

she likewise, but the man was impatient for the party; they stood between the trees down from the house by a wooden fence far beyond which I sat on the lawn facing the dazzling white wall.

My mother seemed to float to my left and behind me old without having grown old remaining young, or I was so young she was young but old to me, the wall was so white it almost blinded me and I sat forward in concentration of posture that made me uncomfortable, my arms were before me my legs stretched out my feet stuck upright in new brown shoes soles on a vertical parallel with the white wall and we all sat in the living room, my sister and her husband, my wife myself, my mother my aunts and childhood friends, there was talking and laughter, later we walked from room to room I was showing myself things I had seen all my life they seemed new, my sister and her husband thought it was interesting they pointed to things and we all moved into the library, I see the molding but the rooms were too clean as we were in a museum of my past and somehow my past was absent and the neat planes and surfaces struck my sister's attention and we seemed lonely in a hollow place, my wife sat by the fire in the living room I stood beside my sister and her husband and as I imitated a man the street my mother burst into laughter I was twelve and thirty three I dug my shoes into the ground I must say something to make her laugh I must say something to make her laugh and I became angry my blood boiled I glared at my feet side by side before the blazing white house, if you want me to imitate someone I won't and can't remember well I WILL! I screamed and laughed and mother laughed without gusto and we all sat around and reclined on the ground no on the lawn under the trees the white sidewalk ran from the step to the street the grass was lovely and evenly cut it was a beautiful day, my mother was there, my wife, my friend Loren, I was all my ages, I pointed up and cried, Look! Look!

It was in the sky.

A huge iron gasket with turbine engine and hollow in the center glided over the trees, wavered and stopped; it hung, huge above the trees, just out of my reach, and an object emerged from it, and I watched it drift down through leaves, and stop, and tremble mid air. The object was about a yard long, narrow, like a baton; a floating arrow in the sky, above the trees, pointed toward mountains as the baton floated by my face—I lunged for it, and missed grumbling, and it was a thinking silver rod floating to Loren who grinned, and as I angrily growled how in hell do you catch 'em? Like this! he laughed and slid his hand out and missed it, well, he said, it isn't so easy; it tilted up, and then drifted off, and levelled out, and floating upwards slanted over the treetops and out of sight.

I climbed the stairs into the Saturday City, and knocked on the door, it was the night of the Italian Carnival, she was dressing, her body, I was late, I touched her and years later dreamed that touch with the same touch I missed the trees, and the hill and the river of dark torpor and I had dawdled among those trees, well, how many times, back and forth, building my dreams in dreams, and anyway, I spoke to them and they already knew me, they implied I mean, they had never met me, they greeted me as if I had and were all of them and had met me, the streetcar took me all the way into Kirkwood, Missouri like words before they are words, and I know her, literally like I know my dreams, and I know my dreams and I know my life, tonight I argued—when I—Barbara calls for me to come to bed, come to bed.

[18]

"Come to bed," etc etc the river and the trees, the basketball game and the glacier above; it is late at night; it is late, and I feel the chill in my life.

* * *

The three flat parcels and the folding Japanese lamps lay on the bed of the flower waggon in front of the store that night, important numbers relating to important things surrounding each parcel—each number or combination of numbers belonged to the parcels in collections and singly with power, a thousand in one, and I worked with the combinations reacting without knowing the facts, the parcels seemed to represent alternatives to a series of persons with sense in the numbers from the parcels, and if I could get the combinations to apply to the sense of one of the thousand in one series the mystery would be solved, I was sure she was the one, she seemed so perfectly placed, but he appeared, as I stood by the waggon, he said something, I saw the answer in the shadowy thing near me, I, frightened in its simple combination, panicked that I had been so obviously complicated.

We used to call her Baby Carol—I did with endearment wit and a guilty jealous cattiness, and when my uncle and aunt drove down from Peoria with their daughter Carol to visit us on weekends, our house seemed to me to fill with Carol and when her mother, motherly catty called her Baby Carol, Carol readily enough got named, and she thus became a pretty scapegoat.

Now we are grown up and the other day I received some photos in the mail, colored snaps of my aunts standing in the front yard smiling and puzzled in their age, and—I saw a photo of Carol with them, and then one of her alone in the yard; she must have driven down alone from Peoria to visit; and she looks like them. Her shoulders are slack and her dress hangs down her twenty two year old body. Her new car shines powerfully in the street behind her but she is self-conscious—being there—in virginity and loneliness in the company of maids a half century older than herself, she doesn't know what to do about herself. The photo is on my desk now, in my mind strongly contrasted with my memory of her once blooming flesh—now vanished, and the old prefix hangs in the air of the old trees and lawns by the old unchanged street where she played when she visited us those years before; the sun is over her head, strangely, so strangely I am shocked, in the perception there is no shadow at her heels, she casts no shadow

Died at 10 p.m. born in Peoria Jan. 7, 1938, surviving her are her husband, and her parents, and three sons Eric Christian, Mark and Frederick Lewis. She donated her body to cancer research at Duke University.

Onion soup 30¢

# THE SENTRY

*In Memory of Betty Olson*

THE SENTRY was stationed off the road at the bottom of the hill, watching for Nazi tanks, he had been there since early morning, now it was early afternoon and the sky was dusty blue in the tops of German trees, a thick nature smell circulated on the summer air and the sentry ate his rations and settled comfortably in the small hollow of leaves.

He was poorly hidden, he knew it, he was visible from the waist up, but he couldn't concentrate on it, he absorbed the air of the German forest and ate, he smoked a cigarette and later rose and went to the bathroom behind some bushes, he returned and sat oddly upright in the small hollow, and watched the road. It was a level and narrow dirt road running through the forest, and he watched it, commanding a view of some forty yards, straight open road, from about twenty yards to the side, time had passed and he had memorised the stillness of air over the road, he would know the moment it was broken. The troopship had risen into the sky, descended into an abyss flanked by watery cliffs—his memory of it was excellent, he had written her a letter then, apologizing for his failure to meet her, in his heart he felt he had avoided his responsibility of her, he did love her but not as much as he was afraid of a life with her, but he was disturbed by his neglect of her, he had told her he would come and she had waited, then he was on the troopship to Europe writing her he was sorry, he was tormented by his selfish irresponsibility, he felt he cared for himself regardless of her, he should have at least written or phoned her, so, he wrote her a letter in his mind.

"I am in Germany watching a road for Nazi tanks, it is a lovely day, the sky is so deep it mingles with the leaves and I feel I am in the sky, I think of you for the ten thousandth time, and wish I could tell you how sorry I am." The thought of her face and her warm eyes now made him guilty and haunted his sense of what he thought he should be, upsetting a hope for safety, he was a failure as a man, the tank banged into view with a rumpled Nazi soldier on top, it moved slowly, the sentry looked at the Nazi, their eyes met, their eyes held on each other the sentry's mind clicking off procedure to follow, yet remained still, he was poised in perception, the picture rose in his mind clearly and perfectly, like a photograph, it registered the figure of the Nazi soldier in a dusty and unkempt uniform sitting on the tank moving down a road looking at him, their existence was vivid, the sentry did not relay the information on his walkie-talkie because he would not distort the perception and the tank was gone, its racket faded on the afternoon air; that night the sentry rejoined his company, he reported he had seen nothing and the next morning they advanced deeper into the war.

# CLASSICAL SYMPHONY

*for Laubies*

HE STOOD by the linotype watching its action while the operator typed. An old fascination. One of the girls came down the aisle saying Truman ought to be in any minute. "You going to see Harry?"

"Yeah." Jack closed one eye slowly: "Him and Mack Arthur."

"Aw—no," the girl said. "Harry Truman's coming in on the three seventeen, taking a limousine into Saint Louis."

"How come he doesn't get off at Union Station?"

"He's coming in from Kansas City, Globe says he wants to see some friends along the way."

Jack said: "Probably has 'em from Clayton on."

The man at the linotype tipped his head back and muttered oh yeah.

He went back to typing, saying, "Harry Truman." Then he laughed. The girl grinned. One of the Jones boys angled between presses and tables covered with type, some proof sheets in his hand, said hello to Jack—

"Going to see Harry?"

Jack laughed. "Wouldn't miss it!"

About five after three the man turned off the light above the linotype keyboard. He shut off the machine, stood up and stretched. The girl who had spoken with Jack finished distributing type, and the Jones boys, the janitor, the editor and Jack went through the front office and out the street door, crossed the asphalt street, cut between a line of trees and walked a narrow expanse of grass that ran parallel with the railroad tracks. A few people had gathered, and were standing around talking and smiling. The group from the town newspaper joined them.

The railroad station was on their left, about fifty yards away, and on their right, just their side of the bridge which was almost opposite the newspaper office, was the cabstand, and cabs pulled in and out, and at three twelve a shiny black Cadillac slipped into the parking area, a man at the wheel cut the engine and another man, beside him, rolled the window down and looked out. A man in the back seat took off his hat.

A distant whistle sounded; they looked west towards the bridge and heard another whistle. A moment later the big Missouri Pacific engine roared in under the bridge and ground to a stop in front of the station. Two men got out of the Cadillac. They were dressed in black, they were smiling.

A few people got down from the sparkling Pullman cars, handed luggage to station porters while men and women and children greeted each other, moving over the brick walkway toward the station.

But two men separated from the passengers and began crossing the grass towards the group of townspeople. The two men in black likewise moved away from the Cadillac, toward them.

"Hiya, Harry!" somebody yelled, and the people parted for him. He smiled and nodded, touching the brim of his hat.

"You're all right, Harry!" a man exclaimed. Truman was talking to the man at his side, and then greeted the two men in black who had come to him, and the four moved to the Cadillac. Somebody asked Truman what he thought of Ike now. Truman grinned, people were walking alongside him now, looking at him and smiling, as Truman talked with the two men in black. He walked briskly, his arms moving, and he talked to the men in a knowing and reasonable but altogether friendly manner, inquiring about friends, using first names or nicknames, as he was walking through the grass, and when they reached the car the door was held for him and Truman got in the back seat, the three men got in, there was a pause while the engine started, and as people waved, the black Cadillac pulled into the street, Truman looking out the window pleasantly, smiling and making a gesture a wave in departure, before he sat back in the seat of the moving machine.

Paris lay under a fog. The Eiffel Tower looked like a nail, its tip just visible above the fog. From the foot of the rampart orchards lined off into the distance. Tall, evenly spaced poplars lined the promenade. Her fiancé stood by the poplars; a dark-haired man, a critic in his late thirties. The American soldier on leave from Germany stood beside Mirielle, and they looked into each other's eyes.

She asked him how he liked Paris, how he felt about America, and what the difference was between them. "We don't have your wide open spaces," she said.

"They're all wide open," he said.

He turned his back on Paris, she followed; they leaned against the wall, facing the poplars. "How do you like Germany?" she asked.

"Fine," he said flatly.

"Oh, tell me."

"It is like great paintings in the past that seem to sleep in a dying present; I feel it wherever I go here."

She said she didn't understand and he said, "Well, I resist myself, and Germany and Europe seem like they can get along with the old art."

He sighed at his density, but said, "Listen to me, Mirielle. America has the brightness and glitter of someone who is big and rich and powerful who is trying to skip what can't be skipped, itself, using everything it has to avoid itself, it doesn't glitter inside, inside it's dirtier and more neurotic than it dares believe, it's soaked with guilt and fear for its unsatisfied viciously related hungers which are *never* satisfied, causing a friction sending up great showers of sparks for the whole world to see, and the world cries, 'How wonderful!' "

"You are serious," she said gently.

And oddly, he was flattered. She watched him, and after a silence asked him where he was from. Missouri brought a confusion to her and he smiled, watching her looking into herself; she was involved in a little mystery. Then she looked at him, her broad face bright. "Truman!" she exclaimed.

He wanted to be alone with her, in a quiet room alone with her. With her, as in her eyes he saw the straightaway yes, to extend that day, sexually into sexual night, together in arms.

But the breeze along the promenade brought a premonition of no more than that instant precisely remembered—then the outcry of her name from the dark-haired critic, "Mirielle!" She turned. The man called to her in French, adding in English, "Come on! We go back to Paris!"

# 'ROUND ABOUT MIDNIGHT
*A Christmas Eve Vignette*

*For Miles*

THE NEGRO opened the refrigerator and took out a bottle of coke, opened it and drank. He turned, hearing little feet coming down the steps. The young boy looked at him.

"Hi," the man said.

"Who are you?"

"Who do I look like?"

The boy smiled wryly and shook his head. "Oh no," he said. "I don't believe it."

The Negro man laughed. It was a big laugh with his big belly in it. The boy began to laugh and larger steps came down the stairs. Father.

"Who the hell are you?" Father said.

The Negro laughed again; that big ho ho sound. Father's eyes narrowed. "Okay, Santa, beat it or I call the cops." And Father went into the living room, to the telephone by the Christmas tree; the boy went to the kitchen window and looked out at the falling snow, and then turned back to Santa.

"I knew it was phony," he grinned. "There's no sleigh and reindeer."

Santa laughed and Mother came downstairs. Seeing Santa Claus, she pulled her robe tighter around her throat, went to her son and put her arm around his shoulder and drew him close to her.

"Who are you?" she asked Santa softly; her sleepy eyes were bright, inside, like a distant dot. "What do you want?"

"A coke," said Santa. He burst into a shattering laugh. The

boy also began to laugh. Father came into the room with a gun in his hand. He was pretty nervous. But he said, "Okay, beat it." He lifted the white princess kitchen telephone and dialed, and asked for the police. Santa finished his coke, belched and watched the man talking across the suburbs to a cop at a desk. Father said, as his face reddened, "Yes, Goddamit, some nigger who say he's San—"

Father hung up hard, turned to Santa and began fussing with the safety on the gun.

"What do you think you're doing?" Santa asked. Then he said, "Look, pal, I *won't* hang around here. I've got too much to do; I was just thirsty."

"Come on Dad," said the boy.

"Please leave our house," Mother said. "Now."

Santa scowled, and went in the living room and they followed him. He picked up several brightly wrapped packages and put them in a big bag, and from another bag took out a large package wrapped in black cloth and put it under the Christmas tree. Santa went to the fireplace, the screen had been taken off the hearth, and Santa stood on the hearth in front of the dying flames and began to diminish, and then went into the fireplace and stood on the coals, turned, reached up and pulled both bags in as they diminished to his touch, and then Santa on his toes reached up and replaced the screen.

"Be careful! You're in the fire!" cried the boy.

Santa turned, startled. Then he grinned. "Yeah, the other element," and he laughed. That sound again.

He vanished up the chimney.

The family stood frozen. In a few moments there was a crazy laugh and a racket of hooves on the roof. The boy ran to the front door, unlocked it and ran outside in the snow. There, above, against the falling snow and strange low night, that riding laugh and panting sound of big animals. The boy waved and yelled,

"I'M SORRY SANTA!"

Down from the sky returned ringing mirth, followed by a diminishing roar of laughter, and a song: "PAN AM!"

Then silence; the sky was empty; snow fell.

When the boy went back into the house, Father was standing in the center of the living room. Mother was in a chair, moaning, her hands covering her face. Ashes were strewn around the rug and fluttering from the opened black box—full of ashes—which Father held in his hands, and seeing an edge of a round disc in the ashes, Father lifted it out, and shook the disc, black and shiny, free of ashes, it was a 45 r.p.m. record, Father blew the ashes off the label, it was White Christmas, the singer was Bing Crosby, and across the hole in the center there was a small white card, like a business card, with a black border around the small offset printed message:

*Those were the days, my friend,*

and signed,

*eh?*
*Yrs,*
*Santa:*
*X*

# PROVINCETOWN INTERLUDE

I STOPPED in a tavern on the way home, it was ten to eleven, two men were at the bar shouting and mumbling to each other while three men argued with a woman in a booth and the woman yelled, "Mary Jane Latham is a good person! You don't have any romance left in you, you son of a bitch!" I got a beer with a shot and sat in a booth, the door opened and a small paint-splattered old man with white hair in baggy housepainter's clothes staggered in with his hands out, he was glassy eyed and smiling bitterly, a screwdriver and paint scraper hung out of the bulging big pocket and he zig zagged to the bar and begged the bartender for a drink nothing doing his tab was too high, the old housepainter said he was doing a job which would pay his tab and the bartender gave him a drink and the bagging uniform and bones climbed up on a barstool drinking and mumbling, lit a cigarette and fell silent.

I left near one o'clock realizing on the way I had had more than I thought turning the corner I heard a voice so I turned around again and the little housepainter hardly able to stand, called and waved for me to come to him which I did, he took my arm insisting I come with him and have a nightcap, he thanked me because I had slipped him a couple of dollars at the bar, we walked to the end of the street and turned the corner and crossed a lawn covered with broken children's toys, a midget car, a broken ladder and empty overturned paint buckets. We went into a dark garage of pungent paint in fresh night air. I stood still hearing him smashing into cans and ladders mumbling and clearing his throat cursing the evasive light switch, laughing and complaining, he could never find it, his wife moved it on him, she was a clever one and knew his ways, yet I needn't fear, he was certain she would like me, as much as he did, and one day he would invite me to supper and I would meet her, and his two beautiful daughters, no, only one now, Virginia had just gotten married, she was the artistic one, did I know how to paint? He was a good amateur painter, and one day he would show me one of his pictures, he said, of a clown it was, a woman across town had said it was sure to win a prize, although he suspected her of funny things, she was from New York and when he painted her house for her— he burst into laughter and the lights went on. "I knew I'd find it," his voice said, as I could not see him through the maze of lumber, broken furniture and piles of housepainter's equipment, I edged through and came upon a small clearing on the dirt floor, a board lay across two overturned five gallon paint buckets and a still life of a half pint of rye stood beside two cans of beer all of which he opened and he pointed to a paint can, we sat and he apologized, Fawcett, he said, he didn't have much time, he had to be up by five and out painting, he told me I didn't believe he would be up by five, but he assured me he would, that he was in fact up every morning of the world at five out on the job, he asked me where I lived telling me I was a stranger in town he asked me if I was from New York, yes, well, he said he had a lot of fine friends in New York Christmas cards every year, but he liked me, where did I live, number six Roseland! Roseland! Which number? Six! and he said,

"Six! Why that's the house Doris Fisher used to have!"

Did you ever hear of Doris Fisher—you mean you haven't heard of—Ha! I grinned and shook my head and sipped the rye and drank some beer and he said,

"Doris Fisher was a great friend of Eugene O'Neill's, and when Doris Fisher gave a party it was something." The little housepainter burst into laughter, slapped his knee and shook his head and said she was really something, Eugene O'Neill was a great writer, didn't I think so? Yes, and he looked at me and said Fawcett—he would invite me to supper, he said, and he had a way of saying oh-oh under his breath when he thought of his wife, his eyes got bright and devilish and he looked at me and said oh-oh and laughed and whispered, "Oh-boy!" He positively urged me to help myself to the liquor, which I did, and when it was gone we finished the beer and I invited him to come over soon, and see my house, I told him I had bought it and he looked at me wide eyed for a moment, he said it was about time somebody bought that place, if I ever needed any help let him know, he sure would help, "I can do anything," he said, the house had a good foundation, the windows were all in line, he hadn't had a close look at it for years, but the last time he had been under it it was in good shape, it's a good house, he said, and he asked me a little how I was painting it. I answered him and his admiration for me increased, we finished the last gulp of beer and went into the yard, he said goodnight Fawcett, and silently wove his way ghostlike between the debris to a door which he opened and quietly vanished into—I went into the street, and as the town was closed I went for a walk on the beach. I sat on the sand and watched the night ocean; Spain across the water.

And I woke facing the initial traces of dawn. The air was clear and the sea smell somewhat stunned me. I began home.

I passed some beach houses, gray in dawn, small and old and gray and dark inside and as I walked along the highway the wind had a character of oblivion, but turning a bend I saw a distant square light of window on the ground floor of a gray house against a large dark gray dune off the shoulder of the highway and as I passed I looked in, a big guy with thin blonde hair cut like a professional soldier's was sitting at a piano, his skull was square, he had a distracted look, a cow lick stuck up, he was powerfully built and self-conscious and a girl was standing beside him looking down at him. He was playing and looking at the keyboard and then up to her—her long dark hair, her dark eyes, he was singing, the window was open, and I heard the pitch.

"When I fall in love," he sang huskily, "it will be forever," and he paused, "or I'll never fall in love;" he struck the keys with meaning and became gentle in his feeling for the song, softly working the melody with his right hand and chording with his left, yet occasionally using his right hand alone, he looked up at her; "In a restless world like this is," he began, "love is ended before it's begun," and he tipped his head to one side with a style of meaning as he sang, she, long dark hair, etc., comprehending the man that sang to her in front of her, in a kind of effort to at last achieve somebody else's tableau—the one that worked—he was singing and making music for her and she waited for him to make up her mind about what of him she would see, she smiled down at him, she was waiting, and "and too many moonlight kisses," and drifting, he appeared he would play it her way, he would wait and see how he would see himself, he had seen her seeing him, he was showing her how he wanted her to see and take him, he played softly, "seem to melt in the light," he began to gather his style and meaning into his upturned face, "of the sun;" he improvised a while, and brought the song to its climax across a world in a house on the sand by the sea. She bent to him, and they kissed.

As I crossed my yard I heard a whisper, no! And then, No! And then, harshly: "Aw—"

"No!"

"Why!"

"I—"

Footsteps ran along a walk, a gate slammed and running steps vanished upward, a door banged shut, and after a second the birds, who had been startled, began singing, and I went inside, and went to bed, wondering if I had my tableau to act out hoping it looked like the one somebody else pulled off that worked, and in a sense I gave up, of course I did, so I gave up the fight, and I smiled, because just as she bent to kiss him, I swore I saw him look up, just for a second, like he was looking in a kind of glass, to see if the reflection looked like the face that got her to come up there and listen to him in the first place.

JEANETTE'S EYES glistened but there was a hardness inside them, she smiled Dick grinned, they touched hands. Dick gazed at the baby and thought about himself and feared Jeanette and wondered what would become of the attitude at home, concerning him.

He left the hospital. He walked down the steps to his car; he drove down the highway. She would be home tomorrow. The doctor said so, and Dick contemplated tomorrow and the certainty of Jeanette's eternal motherhood and inner separation from him, as she would need him he realized the meaning of his day by day routine in terms of cash necessity, what had been before and the longing for the baby was now reality and he felt his sense of identity start its glacial move away from polar center of true ego and consciousness. He parked the car and got out and walked up the steps to the house; unlocked the door; the dog jumped up on him and he patted the dog. He fed him; he looked around the house for the last time of his own again feeling his identity slipping away and he felt like he in a way felt mother felt when he must have stood there in her and in that way standing self feet on the floor Dick leaned out to bridge the distance between his mother his wife and himself, he touched the chair that meant coming home and sitting after work looking over the television listings, the chair was him, too, and he looked over the room over his life hearing the future voices taking care of the child cranky talking chattering neighbors and Dick began talking and looking over the room, the front window was the girl's outer borderline of the inside world in this living room, a schoolteacher scolded his girl Dick's face dropped speaking to the teacher tense that he must assert himself to defend—proud that he would hold his little girl to his side he would he was a tall handsome that girl at work had smiled how he wanted to go into her in his arms Jeanette had given Dick her hand as if guns had gone off killed first in marriage second in loneliness and he longed for an evil he hadn't experienced, longed for the comfort of his dearest mother-air he missed driving to the station he had gotten on the commuter train today looking down at the baby there in his mind the whistle blew, goodbye, he called looking out the window at himself by the street, goodbye! dearest unfound staring at the ceiling in the obligation of fatherhood and end of himself as he understood himself wanting him, single X never had, in the eyes of others—Jeanette—*like* the eyes of others to Jeanette the baby would appear in Jeanette making her happy and busy and the train disappeared over the horizon, tears came and he sat forward head in hands, moving away.

That night in bed in the silent house Dick stammered farewell to himself and from the quiet suburban street came the distant sound of the city and other things going on elsewhere, and from the darkness swarming around his temples light flashed, his arms opened to the absence of perceptive questions and answers, and he wept again starving lonely moving vastly away toward himself he stumbled into sleep and dreams of his job the money the duty selfishness hypocrisy misunderstanding running down his arms into a completed fist.

# DREAM

ON AN ASPHALT ROAD lined with trees he followed a slow circle upwards towards the cabin. There it was. He walked up the hill seeing it down, into Provincetown in his part of what the hill made, and he lost it. But they were all there, just as before, in the long tunnels, the corridors and caverns of memory, and he reaffirmed his desire to have the meal on the way up and into the deep yet fair confrontation on the hill. Christ! That house on the hill! It was as if—as if you were terrified and fell as far as falling could take you, and of itself be, passing the customs on Staten Island to get in you wind up alongside a body on the way to Provincetown and that house hangs up above where he, and she is, you go into the mountains of Pennsylvania beyond the softball park that mother left you (we are all artists) I went up the darkest road into the most vertical and rigid city hunting through cardboard streets like stone for your great hand—up the road I went and the buses and firetrucks and cars and cabs roared downhill. For a moment we lived in that cabin and then we were to be again later, absolutely together I saw in the corner of our shack, which was by our bed, the telephone, and I knew, just as surely as I had come the weary journey across this country I was on my way home, and I ran down the corridor in high school, out the side door and on an angle towards the trees and the game in uproar I retreated, and I was such a sucker while those guys made out with their lives, and I looked out the windows on the bus and the trees and lawns zip by I came out of the forest seeing the long trip up the side of the mountain literally going right up the path to meet her, and she wasn't there.

There was never before to me, and nowhere in me, and nowhere to appear what her was, already sleepy and yet the most extraordinarily awake on the jukebox the luckiest people in the world.

Onion soup: 30¢.

> *people who need, are the*
> *in the, in the, a feeling deep*
> *in your, no more, in this*
> *world*

# HELLO, SID?

*For Larry, for Betty Brooks, Lopez,
Leon Matthews, and Jim Herndon*

*The chaplain was short and stout. His face was white and
creamy and chubby, black rimmed glasses were conspicuous;
as he addressed the men he from time to time took the glasses
off and rubbed thumb and forefinger on the little pink spots on
either side of the bridge of his nose; sharp nose. He had sleek
blonde hair on the sides of his bald head, and his mouth was
little, and tight. His glancing eyes were light colored and
moved fast, even as he began with a prayer, which was then
followed by his long monologue.*

*How tiny we are in this relative universe, we are microbes
on a grain of dirt warmed by a pumpkin sun in a scale beyond
our comprehension, whole galaxies light years apart, and we,
with our insignificant little problems—befitting our tinyness—
complain, here, in this wonder of God's garden. But God hears.
Praise God. He is All, and praise Jesus, His Son, Who came
down to help, and we killed Him—yet He died for us. A mystery born in His power to forgive us, and we are everlastingly
guilty, that the Son of God be sacrificed to, and slain by, specks
of humanity on infinity's plain—pray for redemption. Amen.*

I

Menedez ordered beer, Bozo ordered Scotch and soda, J. M.
Davis ordered rye with a water chaser. When Katrina brought
them the boys were smoking and talking. They paid her and

[39]

she thanked them.

"Katrina baby," said J. M. Davis, "in ten minutes bring the same."

"O.K." she said.

"Five," Bozo smiled. "In five minutes."

"Shoor," she said, walking away.

"Deutsch chicks talking English. In the EMClub. Funny," Menedez said. He held up his glass; J. M. Davis and Bozo did the same. "Prost," Menedez said.

An hour later they stood by J. M. Davis's wall locker waiting for him to put his civvies on.

"Come on," Menedez said.

J. M. Davis looked up. "You got a worry, Jim?"

"Let's go," Menedez said.

J. M. Davis zipped up his fly. He said he was ready.

"We should stop by the club for a short one before we go."

"Yes, Bozo," cryptic J. M. Davis smiled.

They went down the hall and checked out through the orderly room. Packer was on CQ; he was a son of a bitch. Packer.

"Midnight, Davis," Packer. "Not ten after."

"Yeah," cryptically.

They left. They stopped by the EMClub and had a drink, then another, then one for the road to Heidelberg.

"What are you drinking, Bozo?" J. M. Davis asked.

"Scotch."

"What's it in?"

Bozo smiled. "Me."

J. M. Davis grinned. Menedez laughed. "Tough."

The place was the size of a large ballroom and it had great murals, scenes of old Heidelberg, on the walls. A German band near the entrance played oompa umpa. The bar was to the right of the bandstand and the tables stretched across the huge floor to fill the place. At the tables, German girls. Waiting for American soldiers.

Bozo and Menedez and J. M. Davis came in and right away Menedez saw his old lady. Maria joined them, said hello to Bozo and nodded to J. M. Davis. He was uncomfortable. She didn't like Negroes.

"Hey, Bo," he said. "Let's beat it."

"Menedez," Bozo said. "You stick here with Maria, Davis and I are cutting out."

"O.K.," Menedez said. "I know where." Maria said goodbye to Bozo; J. M. Davis had gone and Bozo joined him in the dark alley. "Where to," J. M. Davis said. "They don't dig me in there."

"Well, Menedez had to meet his old lady. How about making 54?"

J. M. Davis laughed and took Bozo's arm.

"Nice," he said softly. Cryptic. "Nice. Nice pal: you: Bozo."


54 was behind a big barn type barn door in the center of a very dark and narrow alley. They both had the special Club 54 passes, as Bozo had gotten one for J. M. Davis saying he was a musician; he wasn't. Germans think all Negroes are musicians. The slot in the door opened when Bozo knocked; an eye peered out and said in German, let's see your passes. They had them ready. The door swung back and they went in. Bozo's friend, Lucky, an American musician in exile from the States, no soldier, was behind the table checking passes; "Hi, man," he said to them, standing up. His chick, a pretty German girl named Christina stayed in her chair and smiled at J. M. Davis and Bozo. Lucky shook hands with both soldier friends.

"What's happening tonight?" asked Bozo.

"Nothing," Lucky said. Then he smiled. "Same shit."

J. M. Davis grinned. "Tough cat: you: Lucky."

"Go down and take a look," Lucky said, sitting down.

The passage down was circular, with steps like white dominoes, held in suspension by long vertical wires; the steps corkscrewed to a lower floor, ending about three feet from the bar. 54 was a small place; an old winecellar whitewashed and converted into a jazz hole. Opposite the bar, not far down the room, was the bandstand. Another little room, like a tunnel in the wall, also whitewashed, angled off from the bandstand. The chairs and tables had their legs sawed off and were like the furniture in a dream, or some kind of regressive underground kindergarten.

Ben Royal was off from Headquarters and blowing the most miserable trumpet anybody ever blew, and beside him, a tall thin Negro named Sanford, also from Headquarters, was playing a terrible tenor and in the back of that a German fellow was playing drums with a beat like how grandmother gave you silver dollars: one at a time. His name was —son something. Erickson, Karlson, maybe. Karlson. Karlson was sitting in because Abe was on leave, Ben Royal said. Abe was blowing with a group in Paris. "I got a card from Abe." Nobody had seen Sam Funny so there was no bass. A very white guy named Leo was playing piano. He was new, had just arrived from the States with fresh stories about Bird at the Open Door, Miles sounded weak (Bozo winced), and he had a pal he knew once who had seen Tristano; new stuff with flutes and all that crap was going on on the West Coast, Leo said, out of his pale face . . . but as he played now, J. M. Davis laughed because Leo had to wait for Ben Royal and Sanford to blow all their notes away so he could play something. Bozo and J. M. Davis each got a beer and sat at a table near the bar, their knees above the tabletop. Ben Royal finished his tired bit and said Hi man, and J. M. Davis and Bozo smiled back and said the name. Soon the set was over and everybody stepped down, a step, off the stand, a small stand, and crossed to Bozo and J. M. Davis. Ben Royal and Sanford and Leo and Karlson sat down, there was nobody else they knew—a German couple was off in the corner so hung up on each other it could have been Wayne King they wouldn't know. Wayne King! "Man," Sanford said, "I met a great chick last night." J. M. Davis cleared his throat.

Leo said,

"I'm going up and blow alone."

He went to the stand, sat at the piano and began to play; two big Germans came down the steps with two fine blondes; one of them spotted Bozo and tossed him a cool Deutsch wink. J. M. Davis laughed and snapped his fingers.

"Yeah: you: Bozo."

"Tough chick," Bozo grinned. "Would you like to meet her?"

J. M. Davis frowned and dropped his eyes. "Nix," he said. "You go ahead, Bo, I have to cut back soon anyhow."

Bozo breathed in and out and looked at Leo. Leo was playing April In Paris.

"Leo," he said. "Leo, play something else. Play Move."

Leo began to play Move.

"Nice," J. M. Davis said. Ben Royal, Sanford and Karlson got up and went to the bar. Bozo turned to him and put his hand on his wrist.

"Lay off that old stuff," he said. They looked at each other. "Hello." The blonde who had winked at Bozo was standing behind him. Hello, she had said.

"May I join you?"

"Sure," Bozo said.

She sat between them.

"J. M. Davis, this is Trudy Braun."

Trudy laughed. Bozo said: "See? I did remember." Trudy said she was glad to meet J. M. Davis.

"Is that really your name? J. M.?"

"Yeah. A nickname. My pals Menedez and Bozo laid it on me—Jefferson Maybe."

"Ach—the name ist: Davis? Then?"

"Right."

Her eyes brightened.

"Gott! Right!—But who is Jefferson Maybe—ahh yes . . . the name is Maybe. Maybe Davis and they call you Jefferson. A pun? Yess. Maybe Jefferson? Maybe Thomas Jefferson? Your American hero; second president? Yes. Ahhh. That is sweet."

She smiled.

"Yeah," J. M. Davis said. "Maybe Jeff Davis."

She frowned.

Bozo cackled and grinned to J. M. Davis. "You're sunk."

"What is sunk?"

"Finis," Bozo said.

"Kaput," J. M. Davis smiled. "Tough chick."

"Ach: kaput? Kaput! KAPUT! Gott!" She burst into laughter and Leo stopped playing. Bozo and J. M. Davis were grinning. Sanford sat down with them and looked at Trudy. She looked at him.

"Hello," she said.

"Trudy, meet Sanford," Bozo said.

"Hello Herr Sanford, what is tough chick. Me?"

"Yeah," Sanford said. "Too much."

"Ahh, too much I know."

"Cool," Sanford said. He drank beer and watched her. J. M. Davis looked at Bozo.

[44]

Trudy stood up.

"Now I go. Listen to me for one moment, please. I come with friends and will now join them again. Bozo and I are friends because he comes to the library where I work. At the desk I work. It is an American Army Library. Sometime you can come? J. M. Davis? I will show you around it. It would be for you fun. It has been nice meeting you, and Herr Sanford and you too, again, dear Bozo."

"Who the hell was that?" Leo asked, sitting down. He was excited. "Man," he finished.

"God, my lip is shot," Ben Royal said, sitting down. He had a big bottle of beer in his hand. He was rubbing his lip. He looked angry. "I got a fucking feverblister."

"Quit eatin' it," Sanford said.

"Dogs smell their own shit first," Ben said.

"Bow wow," Sanford grinned.

A half an hour later music lurched along—several people sat around, talking and drinking; Bozo and J. M. Davis went to the bar, passing Trudy's table. The other girl was almost as lovely. Her hair was cut choppy, Trudy's was long and soft; she was more pale than Trudy, but her eyes were very bright. Trudy's eyes were moody, more dark. Bozo and J. M. Davis got beers and as they went back Trudy caught them.

"Please, meet my friends," she said.

Everyone stood up. Even the girl.

"J. M. Davis and Bozo—ach, Bozo, schoen Bozo, this is Ingrid Brecht, Hans and Frederich Bremen."

They shook hands. Ingrid had a nice hand.

Hans Bremen asked if they would join them. Bozo looked at J. M. Davis.

"Sure," J. M. Davis said.

As they sat down about fifteen people came down around

down the steps and Ben Royal and Leo and Sanford and Karlson began playing different songs the same way; it sounded good to the people coming in . . . Ben played the same riff on Tea for Two that he did on My Funny Valentine, Speak Low, The Lady Is A Tramp and almost anything else, and towards the end of the evening when everybody was stoned Sanford played Danny Boy till the tears ran out of your ears: he had played it all night and now he was playing it by itself—so they all swung in on I've Got You Under My Skin and Bozo told Trudy they were playing it for her.

"Playing what?" she asked.

"That song," J. M. Davis said.

"What is its name?"

"I've Got You Under My Skin," Ingrid chirped. J. M. Davis' eyebrows went up. "Hey," he said.

"I have home an album of Erroll Garner!" she sang. Before he could act like he couldn't (he could) help it, J. M. Davis said he would like to hear it. Sometime.

"Please do," she said nicely. "Do you want to come tonight? We could have a party."

"Tough," J. M. Davis growled. "God damned tough night: this. Man," he complained, wrenching the words out: "I can't make it. I can't make a tough scene."

"I don't follow—" said Ingrid.

"Oh *man*," J. M. Davis said.

Bozo was laughing.

Five German guys and two girls came circling down the steps, followed by three Stateside cats, one with a horn case, and the other two with cat-like expressions like 'I can play too'.

Ben Royal yelled something; it turned out this guy was Stan Nestle, and he was supposed to be something; Ben Royal was always saying Stan was great. That meant Stan might be able to play.

Stan Nestle mumbled something, like hello.

Stan Nestle undid the latches on his case in front of everybody and took out the golden horn and put in the mouthpiece. He oiled all the valves, wiped the horn off and quietly played with his back to the band; then he stepped up and joined Ben Royal. Arnold Paul came down the steps with his bass. Arnold Paul was laughing and three German chicks clustered and beamed around him. J. M. Davis had a big grin. Arnold was tall and thin and stooped; he wore dark clothes, dark glasses, goatee & shrugging expression. Discharged in France he had stayed, in Europe, and was now having a great ball. Bozo and the girls and their escorts watched; Arnold and J. M. Davis said, "Hi, baby, what's happening?" gave each other some soft skin and Arnold, followed by the girls, shuffled to the stand and began unpacking his bass. Nobody was listening to Stan Nestle.

"Who is that?" Ingrid asked.

"Arnold Paul," Bozo said. He glanced at J. M. Davis.

J. M. Davis smiled; "Don't be jealous, Bo," he said. "You and me: tight." He held crossed fingers in the air. The two girls and the two men laughed at them.

A girl came down the steps and looked the place over, and went back upstairs.

Bozo finished his beer. "I'm going to get drunk."

"Ahh, drunk?"

"Drunk."

He went to the bar and got a beer, returned. Then he apologized. "Would anyone like a drink? I mean—I'll get some."

Two pernods, two goldwassers and one beer. He passed them around in German and sat down.

"What time is it in New York?" Ingrid asked.

"Time for Symphony Sid," J. M. Davis grinned. "My man."

"What time is it anywhere," said Trudy.

"What time is it in New York. A-M-E-R-I-K-A," Ingrid grinned.

"Nighttime," Bozo mumbled.

"My time." J. M. Davis.

"Well," said Hans Bremen. "I think soon we have to leave."

"Leave?" Ingrid asked.

"Nein," Trudy said.

Bozo shook his head. "Spader."

Ingrid said something to Frederich. He nodded.

"Spader means later," Bozo told Trudy. "In German."

"I know," Trudy said.

"I know you know," said Bozo. "I knew it all the time."

Arnold Paul took off and everybody got quiet and listened.

Ben Royal came off the stand laughing and shaking his head. He sat with the German guys and girls that had just arrived.

Lucky came down the corkscrew staircase and crossed to Bozo, found a chair and sat down, lit a cigarette, a German smoke, got up and got a beer, returned. He smiled at Bozo.

"Wild music," he said.

"Um," Bozo swallowed. He stood up and said if anyone wanted a drink he would get it with their money.

"Man," J. M. Davis cautioned, taking his sleeve. "Go easy. This is a scene, but cool it. You know. It's early."

Bozo laughed and staggered a little.

"NEW YORK!" he shouted.

Frederich Bremen laughed and glanced at his watch. The girls were laughing and Hans smiled, lit a cigarette, then offered them around. Ingrid took one. Zuban. He held the light for her. Bozo watched all this. He staggered leisurely and wandered off for a beer; he stood at the bar and finished the one he had, got another and returned, sat down drinking.

"It was a long walk," he said. "Germany is beautiful."

"Where did you go?" Lucky asked. Smiling.

"I don't know," Bozo said, "but it was somewhere."

J. M. Davis said, "Who turned you on, baby?" He finished his beer.

"J. M., would you get two more pernods for us?"

"Could you say no?" Bozo grinned.

J. M. Davis laughed, "Not to them."

Bozo stood up. "I'll be back in a moment."

"Where are you going?" asked Trudy, surprised.

Bozo wove up the circular staircase. Trudy watched him. Lucky said something to her in German.

"Ach," she exclaimed. She touched her temple with her finger and laughed.

Three WACs in civvies (who could've guessed), and two Stateside guys came down and looked around, hesitated, looked at each other and went to the bar, got five beers and went to a table. The place was filling up. They sat near a wall, hard not to, and looked wide eyed. They sure had borrowed somebody's passes. They began drinking. Two hours from now, Hans thought bitterly, they'll think they own the place. J. M. Davis returned with two pernods and gave them to the girls, sat down and looked at Lucky.

"Do you live here—in Heidelberg?" he asked.

"Yes," Lucky nodded.

"How? You know. Bo says you don't wear the olive gown . . ."

"I work a little," Lucky explained. "Rents and food are cheap. I have this gig here."

J. M. Davis looked at Lucky. "I'm RA—35 years old—I've

been in thirteen years and busted three times, the last to Private. A drag. You and Bozo and Menedez . . . sweet guys."

He paused, thinking.

"You know what M in my name stands for?"

Lucky shook his head.

"Maybe." J. M. Davis began to laugh.

Time passed.

Bozo came back and couldn't find his seat.

"Ah yes, here you are, you devil."

He sat down and reached for his beer, took a long drink and set it down. He belched.

"Excuse me," said Trudy.

"Bitter," Bozo smiled. He looked at her. "& danke."

The band came off the stand and Christina came down the steps, crossed to Lucky, found a chair and sat beside him. Lucky introduced her to everyone. She was shy. She murmured hello. I wonder, thought Bozo, haphazardly, if she would be that way when she was alone.

Arnold Paul sat with his three chicks. Ben Royal and Leo stood around Trudy's table. Karlson went to the bar. Bozo introduced Leo to everyone. His last name was White.

"Stan Nestle knows Shorty Rogers," Leo White said.

"Crazy," Lucky said.

J. M. Davis explained to Trudy and Ingrid that Shorty Rogers had also played background music for the movie THE WILD ONE starring Marlon Brando. Trudy and Ingrid sighed. Too bad Shorty.

They smiled. Misty eyed.

Leo left, crestfallen. Frederich clapped his hands and called for another drink.

"Another drink?" asked Trudy. "Another drink? You wanted a moment ago to leave."

"First we have a drink," Fred smiled. Lucky smiled. Christina smiled shyly and fiddled with Lucky's wristwatch.

"Can I have a drink?" she asked.

He got up, and returned with vermouth on rocks. Three pairs of German men and women came down the steps. Bozo finished a mouthful of beer and unsteadily set the bottle on the table. J. M. Davis rose to get two more but Fred called him back.

"J. M.!—Zw—two, goldwasser, please?"

Bozo stood up and cleared his throat.

"Yes," he said. He joined J. M. Davis at the bar. The bar was getting crowded.

"Have you known Bozo and J. M. long?" Trudy asked Lucky in German. He nodded, answered, in German, that he had met J. M. Davis a few months before but had known Bozo in the States. J. M. Davis and Bozo returned with drinks and sat down.

Bozo took a long drink, put the bottle down and bent over, putting both hands against his temples. He felt his stomach rise. He looked up. His eyes were filled with tears. Lucky smiled.

"You can't drink it like it's Budweiser."

"I'm hip," Bozo mumbled.

Time passed.

"Life in America must be unique," Trudy announced. She fiddled with her hair.

"It is," Lucky smiled. "Like in Germany."

"Ach," whispered Trudy. Christina laughed like a loud gnat and sipped her drink. Bozo mumbled to himself and Trudy turned her drink around and around, just an inch in front of her pretty knees. The band went up on the stand and began to play How About You. Bozo sighed and began to sing; J. M.

Davis sighed; Lucky drank. Trudy told Hans to get her another pernod. He did. More people arrived.

". . . good books, can't get my fill!" Bozo sang.

Lucky went for a beer and another vermouth. "Get me a pernod, please?" Ingrid asked. Lucky said sure, took some money from Fred and went into the crowd around the bar.

Now the place was really packed. Some twenty people were at the bar and every table was full; the center aisle was crowded and more came down the steps. The band wasn't playing very well but it was loud and people were getting drunk.

"HOW ABOUT YOU?" Bozo shouted. "Hey baby," he whispered to Trudy, "You're my dreamboat. May I sail away on you?"

She smiled.

"You're drunk."

"Will you marry me, Trudy?"

"No."

"Why not?"

"Because you're not rich. I thought all Americans were rich."

"I thought all Germans were fat." He looked at her. "I'm rich in other ways."

"No doubt," Trudy smiled, "but I can't live the rest of my life in bed."

"All right. After our honeymoon, we'll get divorced."

As Lucky sat down Bozo stood up and threw out his chest—pitched forward—Lucky and J. M. Davis caught him before he hit the table. Everyone helped him up.

"That was close, my friends," Bozo said. "I was going to ask anybeer if they wanted any. Body? Ah, a spoonerism. My lovely continental ladies, do you know what is a spoonerism?

No. Well, Spooner—Edward? Spooner was a professor at Oxford. England. British. Spooner. Boxford. And he once told his students: "Uk the farmy."

Bozo rose and staggered into the crowd humming How About You. The band was playing Moonlight In Vermont and Sanford was blowing Danny Boy. Stan Nestle came on too fast and Ben Royal stood by smiling, waiting to blur on. Christina was whispering to Lucky. J. M. Davis and Trudy and Ingrid and Hans and Fred were talking and time passed. Bozo came back, sat down and looked around the table. The beer bottle swayed in his hand and Trudy straightened it. Bozo looked at her. Horror. His eyes weren't very straight.

"You're getting very drunk," Trudy said.

"Not me," Bozo blinked. "Let's go do it, Trudy. I love you."

A man edged his way through the crowd and touched Lucky on the shoulder. Christina stood up. The man said something in German and Lucky stood up. They went through the crowd and up the circular steps. The man followed them. His head was shaved on either side and his hair was long on top. He wasn't sober but he wasn't drunk. He was that way all the time. He was the bouncer.

"Save their seats," Bozo said.

The crowd at the bar had increased and the place went roaring on; the music was deafening now because Ben Royal and Stan Nestle were playing scream and shriek and calling it Short Stop. A large German woman bent over Bozo and asked, in German, if she could have that vacant chair? Bozo looked at that Deutsch statue and sighed. He smiled brightly and told her to sit there. GI German. She pretended he was German, and said she would but she was with a great big man. She gestured and pointed. Bozo looked. A big man. Bozo stood up with his beer and pounded his chest.

"Me big too."

"Sit down, Bo," J. M. Davis said.

"My German is lousy," Bozo said to her.

"Lousy?" she asked. "Wass ist—"

"Lousy," said Ingrid.

"Lousy is no good," said Fred. Then he laughed. Very loud. HA HA.

"Ach," the big lady said. She went away.

"Sit down Bozo," J. M. Davis said again.

Bozo sat down. Ingrid asked him when he was going back to the States.

"In 142 days," Bozo said, looking better.

"Will you be glad?"

"I got fifteen mother—fifteen months," J. M. Davis frowned.

"What will you do when you get back?"

"Who."

"You."

"Me," Bozo said. "I want a beer. Jeff, get two, will you—I mean while you're up."

"You get 'em," J. M. Davis said. "I'm stuck."

"O.K." Bozo took money from Hans and gathered bottles and glasses in his arms and like a healthy sardine, he plunged into the rest of the pack. Lucky edged in to him as he was putting everything on the bar. Face to face in the crowd.

"There's a guy upstairs named Menedez says he knows you; he's pretty loaded and has a whore with him. We can't keep him quiet."

"Yeah? Mendy?" Bozo grinned. "Menedez! Let him in. He's straight. He plays tenor."

"Will he play?" Lucky asked.

"He'll play. And something besides Danny Boy."

Lucky laughed and was gone. Male and female shoulders

closed in around Bozo. He spotted a couple of officers from the post and glared at them—they glared back. The girl behind the bar was working like crazy, reading lips and labels and finding different bottles, not always knowing, even the familiar customers. She knew Bozo by face, but didn't recognize him. He ordered in German and she dug around and brought up the two beers, put a shot of pernod in each glass and water to the rim. Too much water. Goldwasser went in small thin glasses. After he paid and got change, he put a beer under each arm and picked up the other four drinks like stacks of chips. He began back to the table saying bitte bitte as he went, slowly, nudging and shoving his way.

"AMIGO ZAPATA!"

Menedez.

Mendy's old lady Maria was happily plastered, grinning wide eyed. Christina sneaked in and sat next to Ingrid; Menedez was next to Bozo and Trudy—Maria took Lucky's chair. He had to stay upstairs, Christina murmured. She looked at Menedez:

"Play if you want. Sanford lends his horn."

"If I were sober I wouldn't. I am drunk," Menedez said.

Maria was laughing excitedly, like a zipper in new denim. Bozo was handing drinks around and getting Hans' change back to him.

"Maria doesn't drink," Menedez laughed. Things were popping in and out of his hands, pieces of paper, pencils, cigarettes, matches, and Bozo watched him unevenly, saying,

"What in hell are you doing?"

"One beer, mother," Menedez answered. "Uno."

"Are you going to play your violin?" J. M. Davis laughed.

"You get the brew, I'll go blow, O.K.?"

J. M. Davis sat back. "Some cat."

Bozo went for the beer.

Menedez was on the stand with Sanford's tenor in his hands, quietly tuning up. He leaned toward Stan Nestle and asked, insultingly:

"What are you playing, mother?"

"Talk of the Town," Stan answered. Cool.

"Gee," said Menedez. He waited for his break.

He played softly at first and then, turning to Arnold Paul and Karlson, he dipped his shoulder conspicuously, and, for an instant, Arnold Paul and Karlson stopped—and Menedez came on like Sonny—Sonny Rollins—who makes great trains run at night. Menedez wailed, powerfully blowing long hard lines; Arnold Paul chopped away obliquely behind him and Leo chorded, sharply, with both hands. Menedez laced it out, one big phrase after another. The place stopped, straightened up and stood on its toes and began to jump. Bozo and J. M. Davis were out of their heads.

Menedez built a doorway for Stan Nestle to come through, but Stan tripped, the house fell and Menedez gave Sanford his horn back, thanked him and walked through an admiring crowd. While Stan Nestle played stump and stumble, Menedez sat down; grinning.

"I feel like I ran a buzzsaw through my mouth."

"More! More!" cried Bozo.

Menedez frowned. "Maybe later." He looked over the table. "Where's my beer? I haven't played since highschool . . . my lip's lousy . . . ah, here."

"Ah, lousy," Ingrid mused. "Lip."

Menedez drank his beer thirstily.

"That is fine," he sighed, belched, drank again and, closing his eyes, put it on the table. Ingrid and Trudy began questioning him about music and Bozo sat back. He looked at the whole scene. Hans and Fred Bremen seemed excited, but confused and tired. J. M. Davis was singing in scat . . . the old wine cellar was jammed. People knelt on the corkscrew staircase and peered through the vertical wires. Men and women talked and drank and laughed. The band played on. And the girls were lovely. Girls, Bozo thought. He looked at Trudy. She had her hands behind her head and her eye on Menedez. Her breasts were pointing right across the table. Bozo sighed. He reached—put his hand on the right one, cupped it. He smiled.

Wonderful.

## II

Menedez walked out of the office and looked at Bozo. "14 days restriction, 7 extra duty."

The Sergeant stepped out of the Captain's office and motioned for Bozo to come in.

"Good luck, Bo," J. M. Davis said.

Bozo walked in and made a salute and was put at ease. The door closed. He waited. After a pause:

"I don't like to do this, Bozante," the Captain said.

Bozo looked serious.

"Where'd you get the shiner?"

"Well . . ."

"How did it start?"

Trudy's breast overcame the memory of Fred's big mitt in his eye. It must have been an easy punch. I'd do it again, Trudy. Trudy baby, weren't you surprised?

"How did it start?"

"A girl, sir, her boyfriend was jealous."

"I see. Well. Where was it?"

"I don't remember, sir." He mentioned a well known tavern. Rodensteiner's. They had agreed on that before. 54 was too good for the Army to bust.

"Were you that drunk?"

"Yes sir."

"Do you drink much?"

"No sir," Bozo lied.

"All right, Bozante. You stay on post for two weeks. The first seven days you'll have extra duty. Report to Sergeant Spaulding in the morning; he'll give you orders."

"Yessir."

"That's all. Sergeant, bring Davis in."

## III

Menedez ordered beer; J. M. Davis ordered rye with a water chaser. Bozo ordered Scotch and soda. They sat in the EM-Club in their fatigues. It was Saturday afternoon. Sunlight streamed through the windows.

"Well," Menedez said, "good luck."

They toasted and drank. Bozo gave Katrina the high sign. She crossed the floor.

"In a couple of minutes, bring the same. O.K.?"

"Shoor," she said. "O.K. Bozo."

Bozo grinned, watching her walk away. J. M. Davis smiled and Menedez laughed. "Hooray for us."

"Not for me," J. M. Davis snickered. "I got two more weeks."

While he laughed ha ha ha Menedez held the glass against his ear and the bottle of beer in front of his mouth. "It ain't no secret why. Hello, Sid? What time is it in New York?" He laughed.

Bozo sang hey Lullaby of Birdland, bent over laughing, and looked up. "Do you think he knows?"

"Sid? Sure—so do I," J. M. Davis laughed. "Time for Trudy's tits. And time for *me*. Time for another drink."

They thirstily finished their drinks.

"KATRINA!" Menedez shouted. "KATRINA SHATZ!" They cracked up. "KOMMEN DO HERE BITTE—"

# THE HIGH & THE MIGHTY

## I

I MET HER in a cut rate store on Highway 66. She was buying a pack of cigarettes and I was waiting my turn beside her. She turned and glanced in my eyes. I saw what you see when you're looking out at the ocean. I got some cigarettes and walked out of the store close to her, and asked her what her name was. She had a steady expression of surprise around her eyes and mouth. She said, pretty coolly, I'm engaged. She got in her convertible and looked at me. I was standing by an outdoor coke machine. Cars raced along 66. She said I could call her, if I wanted, and gave me her name and number. The next afternoon I called, later caught a bus that dropped me off in front of her house. She was on the doorstep.

We used her car, and drove around, had something to eat and ended up out of town in a hotel. Our names and faces focused and wound around us; we breathed the air of it until it was finished and we returned. She to her familiar fellow, me to my familiar world in the rain. She got out of my rented car and ran to the city garage where she had left her own car. I watched her go from me into the color of the city. Somewhere in the traffic I imagined Gershwin's Concerto in F. Goodbye, goodbye. I drove away. I returned to my job at the pool. I was a lifeguard. I sat on a high seat under an umbrella, wearing white swimming trunks, dark glasses and a whistle and watched pretty girls all day long. They had a good time, it was great to them, and while I fulfilled my appointment I also wondered what I was doing from one minute to the next, sitting up there looking over trees at farm houses.

It was a small town in the lower left hand pocket of Missouri and I got hung over there longer than I expected, starting by going to a movie instead of catching the next bus. I left the station and walked along the street. It was one of those midwestern evenings when you don't feel like going on with the trip, around seven o'clock, an hour before things start to get light blue. In June. I should have been in New York. As I walked in the movie house the first show was just ending. I went in and sat down wondering why the manager had chewed on his hand and looked at me like he had, why the flowery woman who took my money and slid me the pink ticket was drunk, and why the boy in the dirty gray suit gave me the popcorn saying,

"Sho. Why not?"

It takes my eyes a little while to get used to darkness and main features, but I sat down on the aisle towards the back of the theatre and watched previews. I began on the popcorn. A while later the hair on my neck was moving around as if there was a sudden chasm behind me. I turned and looked behind me. Nobody there. Nobody was sitting behind me, and in fact nobody was anywhere: back front, either side.

The theatre was empty—except for me and a young blonde usherette who stood by the exit, off to my right. She stared at the floor. That painting by Hopper. Then she looked at me. The music was loud. It was about an airplane and whistling pilots. The point of no return. Something moved in the corner of my eye. The blonde came up the aisle and stopped beside me and said,

"May I sit down?"

"Sure," I said. I moved over a seat and she sat down.

She had a maroon uniform on. In the painting the girl has a maroon uniform on. So my blonde had a maroon uniform on. Her breath smelled like lipstick: strawberry. A young blonde. My breath smelled like popcorn.

"Um," I said. I put my arm around her and she laid her head on my shoulder and sighed.

"What will I do?" she asked. "Nobody comes to the movies."

"Except us," I smiled. I felt her lips on my neck; her cheek moved. She was smiling.

"Except us," she repeated.

"Why don't you quit?" I asked.

She raised her head and looked at me. The movie house wasn't dark at all. From the light of the screen—the bright lights from the interior of the airplane and music—her face was pretty clear. She had an ordinary face that was pale and in good light her eyes would probably be soft blue and they would seem resigned. I didn't find out the facts. The three days that followed saw us together but we didn't talk about our lives. We hardly talked at all, except what flavor ice cream she wanted, or me answering her questions. Like the time we were swimming. It was the next afternoon at the pool in the next town. We hitchhiked over. My suitcase was on its way to New York but the travel bag was still in the locker in the bus station, and hands empty we stood on the road in the hot afternoon and held out our thumbs. A pickup truck was the ride all the way. We got off and walked through town to the pool and I rented suits for us and we went in. There were a lot of people, it was a small pool, and after swimming in between them for a while we had iced coffee at the refreshment pavilion. We sat in wicker chairs and held hands across a sticky roundtopped table the color and scale of a candy lifesaver.

"Where are you from?" she asked. She was so still it seemed

like the words came from someone in the pool. On a hot day like that, beside a swimming pool a thousand miles away from Manhattan, the question was almost unreal.

"New York," I said. I felt like I was lying because she was so silent. Nothing in her face changed.

"Let's go back in," she said.

"Jobs are hard to find," she grinned.

"Then give it up," I said. "Look." I was from New York so I tried to talk that way. Instead I kissed her.

"OK," she said. "Oh baby, I quit."

We cut out through the theatre exit and walked through town. I bought a half pint of cheap bourbon and we walked the highway until we got tired. At a turn we stepped over the crash rail and went down an embankment like Indians, into an orchard. By now it was dark and we were having trouble walking. We sat under an apple tree and I lit a cigarette that lasted three drags. I undid my tie, she unbuttoned her maroon jacket. The orchard slanted off and the smell of green apples was as fresh and keen as the sound when you crack one in half: it lays open: two halves, one in each hand, dark teardrop seeds in the centers.

On a sunlit wall of a tractor factory I wrote our names big, and to the right of my message she made an x and an o, smaller.

After walking in fields and wading in creeks, we were exhausted. Wednesday night we rented a room in town. The next day we went swimming again, getting there in two rides via the route we had taken Monday. We lay on the duckboards by the pool. Quietly, in the hot sun. That night the bus station was full of people waiting to go places. I took my travel bag out of the locker and we sat on a bench and waited. Outside it was getting blue.

"Goodbye baby," she said.

The bus pulled in noisily and about four people got up and began getting on. We were at the end of the line. When it came my turn I gave the driver my ticket and he tore the bottom part off. I had my travel bag in my hand. I didn't know what it was for or what to do with it. Where I was going or why. I put it on the bottom step and glanced at the driver. He got on the bus. I looked in her eyes and we kissed goodbye. I got on the bus, went in back and sat near a window, slid it open. She stood below me, blonde and pale, looking up. Her light blue eyes were still and distant. The bus engine growled and barked. I shoved my arm out the window and she took my hand. We both said it but not out loud. I got my arm back in and the bus began to move. She walked across the street with it and then began to run. GOODBYE BABY. The bus gathered speed and smoked out of town.

The last I saw she was standing on a street corner in her maroon uniform, in the blue Missouri twilight.

# PLAY BALL!

IN MISSOURI, in the summers during the war years, the church softball league was started and Mr. Meredith volunteered to manage the Episcopal team.

He would make a fast team, he said, a team that would move. He coached from third and his face got red and he yelled hoarsely, cheering and giving signals to his boys. When he shuffled his feet: take, when his hands were on his hips: hit and when he spat in the dust, steal.

Run! His gimlet eyes praised fleet feet, strong legs and trim bodies. When he signaled the steal his eyes shot sparks. Palo slid hard into second, hooking the bag, safe. Mr. Meredith clapped his hands and savagely shouted Hit! Hit! Hit!

But they didn't win. And at the end of the first season finished next to last.

The following summer Bozo walked around in left field and watched Mr. Meredith; Bozo was rubbing his hand in his glove hitting it, Mr. Meredith was sitting on the bench. Bozo saw Marjorie Meredith in the stands; pretty. She was with her gang. They laughed and cheered and giggled, and groaned. Her father was coach. Bozo looked in at him. He was afraid of him.

Bozo drew a walk, Mr. Meredith spat in the dust and a moment later Bozo was sitting on the basepath, out. Mr. Meredith's face reddened, his gimlet eyes squeezed, he stepped forward jabbing the air like a fighter, right and left fists hitting air. "I said *run!*" he cried swearing hoarsely. Bozo walked off the diamond and sat on the bench. The girls giggled and made little bleats.

During the next practice Mr. Meredith made Bozo run bases; the team stood on the sidelines of the empty field and watched Bozo run from home to first, from first to second, from second to third and from third sliding clumsily into home. Mr. Meredith said do it again. Again. "Do it again, Bozante," and afterwards again. "Again!" Bozo stumbled around second and lay down at shortstop. Mr. Meredith knelt beside him, "Now get up, you bozo, I'm going to make you *run*." Mr. Meredith pulled Bozo up. "Take third and go into home—RUN!" he yelled.

Bozo ran to third. He rounded third and started towards home with panic in his heart. Mr. Meredith crouched at shortstop his face crimson, screaming "Run! Run!" Bozo slid into home and got up and dusted his pants, walked to the bench, picked up his glove and walked off the field with his head lowered, fist pressed in his glove.

The rest of the team stood in uneasy silence.

Mr. Meredith jabbed the air twice. "Practice over!"

"You promised."
"I can't."
"Why."
"I can't tell you."
"Bozo?"
He looked at his mother. She said, "You gave your word."

Bozo walked across town to help rake leaves at the Merediths'.

The other kids weren't there.

The yard was empty and already raked; heaps of leaves lay in even rows. Bozo stood at the foot of the front walk. Mr. Meredith was in the yard watching him. "Come on over here, Bozante."

"How old are you?"

"Fifteen."

Mr. Meredith smiled. "Hi, Bozo." He laughed, sour breath, Bozo turned his head, Mr. Meredith grabbed Bozo's jaw and turned Bozo's head back and said, "Time you learned how to fight."

Bozo lowered his eyes, whispered, "I'm afraid of you."

Mr. Meredith hit him lightly in the stomach, Bozo bent over and Mr. Meredith pulled him up, "I could've made you bozo you do the loop the loop."

Bozo flushed. Mr. Meredith crouched suddenly and hit Bozo in the chest. He hit Bozo again, and he hit him again, he followed Bozo's stumbling body across the lawn, striking and angrily whispering, "Fight me! Fight!" Then Mr. Meredith stopped and turned.

Mrs. Meredith was in the doorway. She spoke to her husband. "Come here."

Mr. Meredith went slowly to her. She said to Bozo, "We're sorry, Bo, you can go home now."

Mrs. Meredith held the door while her husband passed in front of her, head down. She followed him in and the door closed. Bozo stood on the grass, looking at the closed door. He did not know what to think except that he was afraid of the man, he feared what was in the man, but most of all he feared the process of his own waking into the responsibility to himself, and a melancholy shadow of fear crossed his heart.

P. K. Singleton's boy Royal played shortstop from the beginning. Royal was good, not as good as Palo, but Palo was tops; Palo was always there first, laughing and dancing around on top.

Royal's stocky build, shyness and wan handsomeness gave him style.

In the summer of 1944 Royal's father became manager.

He was a medium sized man with unruly brown hair he had trouble keeping in place, he tried frantically, but except for those times, he watched his team quietly as from a distance. There was P.K. in athletic sneakers, sweat pants and sweat shirt with a pull string. It was P.K. who asked Reverend House to get uniforms for the boys.

There hadn't been any before. White T shirts had been handed out, with EPISCOPAL printed across like summer camp. Khakies or levis and sneakers had completed the uniform. P.K. ordered glossy blue silk caps, light red T shirts with a big black E over the heart and numbers on the backs. The pants were lightweight and light red with zipper flies. There wasn't enough money in the fund for socks and shoes.

At the beginning of that summer, practice began with P.K. calling everyone by number. The team moved around shouting and playing pepper hitting and shagging flies and taking grounders. Then they gathered around P.K. and he briefed them.

"Boys, here's the way I see it." P.K. fought his hair, cleared his throat and gave everybody the eye. "The first thing that makes any team click is spirit. Team spirit. If you don't have team spirit everything falls apart. Reverend House will back that up, right Reverend?"

Reverend House smiled and nodded.

"This is a great game," P.K. went on, "and to win we've got

to play hard and keep our minds on what we're doing. If we make an error we grit our teeth and don't make that error again. We work together. We all work for the team.

"12, when you get a fly out in left, what do you do when there's one man out and a man on second?"

Bozo shifted feet. "Well, I throw to third, or to Royal."

"6," Royal said.

"6—6 comes out and I get it to him, otherwise I get it into —" Bozo walked among the laughing team himself grinning and looking for Harry Bodley's back—"7."

The following week everyone was everyone again without numbers, and by the second game everyone—except Royal— showed without uniforms, wearing their old T shirts with the faded letters EPISCOPAL across the front.

It was a night game; arc lights shone down on the coach with his hand on his son's shoulder.

"Now son . . ." Royal had the bat in his right hand; they were halfway to the plate. Conroy was on third, there was one out and it was the bottom of the fifth, Saint Peter's was ahead four to nothing. "Just wait for it—don't get over-anxious, we want a hit, boy. We want that run!"

Royal nodded. He drew a walk.

Robin Kater went to bat and struck out, Royal was picked off first as he faked a go towards second, the inning was over and Conroy was left on third, Saint Peter's went on to win another shut out another three hitter, they settled more firmly on top.

"What happened, son?"

"I wanted to draw the throw—I thought Conroy would score from third—"

"We're not talking about Conroy, son, we're talking about you. I don't think you were thinking."

"Father, Conroy didn't move. I broke with Robin's swing. Conroy just stood there—I should have gone on to second but when Robin struck out, I hesitated and headed back to first—"

"You wanted to help, is that it?" P.K. paused. "Next time think, son. Think of the rest, not just what you could have done. If you had stayed close to first, we might have done some damage."

"Robin can't hit, Father, and neither can Phelan or Bozo."

There was a pause.

"What does that mean?"

"It was up to me. But Conroy didn't move. I had automatically thought it was up to me, then—I couldn't stand there—trapped—"

"Son, you took a chance you drew a throw and were put out."

Royal nodded. "I broke too far. I thought Conroy would make a break—if I would have made it back what would you have said to Conroy? Robin struck out and Conroy just *stood* there."

Mother was across the room in her chair, inspecting buttons on a shirt. P.K. and Royal were on the sofa.

"Father, may I use the car tomorrow night?"

"We'll see. Why don't you run up to bed."

Royal stood up. "Yes, Father."

He kissed his mother goodnight and went up the steps and into his room. He undressed, put on pajamas and got in bed and turned on his bedlamp. He read from *The Razor's Edge* until he fell asleep.

Carden backhanded the grounder and flipped it to Royal.

Royal snatched it, crossed the bag for one and whipped it to Marvin on first for two and they came in, tossing their gloves on the grass. It was another night game.

"Son?"

"Yes?"

Bozo was pretending to select a bat while Deerfield teased him. The stands were crowded. Bozo's mother was talking with Reverend House; Mrs. House and daughter Joan were watching Bozo walk to the plate. Joan watched him. Her left eye slowly closed. "Nerves," she whispered.

Bozo was in the batter's box and Deerfield yelled, "You gonna invent a new way to strike out?"

"Questions without answers!" Bozo cried. "The chips are down!"

Hearing laughter and anxious yells, Royal looked at the infield, Bozo was on second base delighted, clapping his hands and laughing. Deerfield was at bat, nobody out, they were behind 7 to 1. Amusement trickled through the stands. The Methodist bench was laughing and shouting at Bozo, and in back of first, on the grass in the dim outer edge of overhead arc lights Negro boys yelled and laughed, "BO! BO!" Deerfield topped a sucker pitch between first and second, the Methodist second baseman made a wrong choice too late, the throw to first was low and Bozo was safe Deerfield grinning on first base.

"Did you hear that?"

"What."

"What P.K. said to Royal—look at Royal—"

"I didn't hear."

Bill Marvin struck out and Franklin walked, and Royal looking more pale was at bat with the bases full and one away. Harlan Davison was on deck. P.K. walked back and forth in front of the bench, ran his hands through his hair, sat down and stood up. Palo was coaching loudly from third.

Everybody's Uncle Curtis the assistant minister had brought his Brownie box camera to the game, and when Royal swung and missed the first pitch the photograph froze the strike for the eternal future—nothing else happened, and they lost it by that score.


She looked at him. He lay beside her on the grass, in the sunshine on Art Hill. They had been to the St. Louis Art Museum.

"You're watching me," he smiled.

"No I'm not," she said she grinned "Yes I am."

He was silent, looking into the sky. Then he stood up, helped her to her feet; they walked down the hill towards the lagoon where colorful boats moved in an Impressionistic distance.

"I'd like to take you for a drive," Royal began, but a high pitched feminine giggle flew up in his throat, cracked and stuck until he was gasping for breath — "but my Father, doesn't like the way I cross second base, as I throw to first—'there is the method of left and right feet,' he said which through lack of thought, I have confused, and as result, the use of his Chevrolet is VERBOTEN!"


Harlan Davison was a big sullen kid with blonde hair. In the summer of 1943, at 13 Harlan had the offhand quality of great sluggers in small towns.

Mr. Davison was a big chested man with soft hair and flat eyes. He walked gracefully with a swing.

Mr. Davison sat in the empty stands watching practice. His

feet were up on the plank below, elbows on the plank behind supporting him, his tie spread over his chest, his chin squared above his chest; his sleeves were rolled and brown sharkskin trousers bagged above black silk socks and dusty brown plain-toe shoes. His snapbrim hat and sport coat hung from a limb on a nearby tree.

"Listen to the coach, kid."

Towards the end of the first summer the Baptists had a new pitcher named Kellon.

The Baptist manager was talking with the woman from the newspaper, they walked over to Mr. Meredith with his scoresheet, shook hands and noted opposing lineups.

"We've got a new boy on the team. Marty Kellon. He'll be pitching."

"Okay," Mr. Meredith said, taking the name. "Got it."

They smiled luck and parted. Kellon delivered—a windmill pitch. "Illegal!" Palo cried, the umpires and both managers and the newspaper woman held a conference making the pitch legal and Mr. Meredith gathered his team around him. "Let 'em have the pitch. When I rub my hands together it means bunt. You know the rest—Harlan?"

"Yeah?"

"Can you hit him?"

Harlan shrugged.

In the first four innings Kellon walked five and struck out ten. Nobody knew how to bunt. Harlan didn't get the bat off his shoulder and the fireballing windmilling Kellon and his Baptist team won 6 to 0.

Mr. Meredith taught them to bunt at the next practice, Palo

tried pitching with the new delivery and because Mr. Meredith asked him, Mr. Davison helped coach.

Two weeks later Saint Peter's had two pitchers better than Kellon and at season's end took league honors.


One cold spring Saturday morning Bozo went over to see if Harlan was home. Bozo walked between patches of snow and when he got to Harlan's house, he stopped at the end of the fence and hid behind a bush.

Mr. Davison breathed vapor. He stood on the dead grass in his shirtsleeves with a ball in his hand. Harlan shivered against the side of the house, bat in his hands. Mr. Davison began to pitch to him overhand, Harlan swinging to chop it on the ground. The ball smacked the house when he missed. His face was drawn and his blue eyes gazed at his father.

Bozo walked, was sacrificed to second and watched the next hitter fly out. Harlan ambled to the plate. Bozo came off the bag and yelled,

"Harlan!"

Harlan stepped out of the batter's box and looked at second base. Bozo clapped his hands and yelled,

"Easy!"

Harlan stepped in. "EASY NOW!" Bozo cried angrily.

The Presbyterian pitcher threw the ball and Bozo broke towards third, but Harlan seemed to pause, he swung easily yet the level whip of his bat toward the ball—starting Harlan racing to first seemed to hold and then release Harlan, pounding toward first as his long swinging hit angled high over shortstop, and as Bozo was around third Harlan leaned around first, Bozo went into score Harlan took a wide turn at second and swung into third on a slant toward home the team had risen from the bench, the Presbyterian left fielder was still chasing the ball, the Episcopal team gathered around the plate cheering and yelling and laughing and calling to Harlan, "Harlan! Harlan!" Bozo ran down the basepath beside Harlan "I knew you would!" he cried, "I knew it!" Harlan glanced furtively into the stands and went into the waiting arms of his team at home plate.

# THE SPLIT-SECOND

IT WAS DAWN, late in Bozo's first New York spring, he was twenty six years old, he was drunk, he was in Central Park heading west along a path. He was depressed, he was broke, he was cold, wet and hungry; fog came in low layers across the park and in gray dawn the trees the soft and pungent earth and the dark shapes of boulders gave the park the air of a dream, and the corners of his lips curved up his face.

His GI boots were wet and his feet cold and wet his levis wet from the knees down, his white shirt was dirty and wrinkled and his olive green corduroy jacket, with its torn pockets and upturned collar—and his hair hanging over the collar—his dirty ivy league cap set aside his head and his unshaven cheeks gave him the appearance, he knew, others—girls had said so—a young English writer, having been drinking all night with friends at the pub, now goes for a drunken and lonely stroll in the park at dawn—on the way home, but Bozo had no place to live, and he put his hands in his pockets, he pulled his arms close to his sides and stooping raised his shoulders shuddering chilled, his boots struck cinders and he stopped—he saw a photograph of himself in his mind in the pub in England, his friends laughing as he joked, the fog billowed around him, trees and boulders vanished. Quickly! He straightened—alert, and on whispering crushes a riding girl on a stepping horse came out of the fog. As she passed her eyes met Bozo's and for a moment held, and then she disappeared into the fog.

Innocence and softness warmth and dearness of gaze, face

and figure, flooded his heart and warmed his blood and his heart beat hard toward the power in her darling cap—set lightly on the side of her head—and her neat fitting jacket, her legs close against the horse her polished boots in the stirrups and her straight spine and precious upright body in the saddle her adorable hair framing her solemnly beautiful face, her living eyes.

Kind and seriously perceptive brown eyes met his own green eyes in split-second perception—contact—forever, then, they were together, forever in that *splitting*.


As this clenched feeling unclenched itself things take their shapes. I remember the girl he lived with a long time ago. This is almost over.

She stood in the grass outside the house and the sun was bright; the air was fresh and warm. But no thing could match the madness in her eyes; she ground her teeth and her tears had to push through her rage.

"I can't tell you, I can't tell you, I can't—"


My wife had seen me talking with him at the soda counter. "Who is he?"

I told her. "After I got out of the Army I hung around a place called The Ten Mile House. I met him there."

"Is he nice?"

"He sees himself from a long way off," I explained. "And he can't get out of this town."


That night he was parked across the street from a theatre; the movie was over, and the crowd spilled out onto the sidewalk. He saw a pretty girl start home. She consulted her watch. He thought he would like to have her.

After the dance he walked her home. They stood on her porch. She smiled and in the moonlight they looked in each other's eyes. They stood apart, looking into each other's eyes. Her eyes were dreamy and her figure seemed to float, but behind her eyes he saw a distant look, and he looked deeper, and yet deeper, and he felt drawn in, and he was moving toward her, feeling her beckon to him, "Bozo," she whispered, and he paused, sensing danger.

Mr. Constant watched from the doorway.

"Bozo," Pamela whispered.

He took her face and neck in his hands and kissed her. "PAMELA!" Mr. Constant yelled, and charged, but Bozo laughed, whispered her name, and ran down the driveway.

Really into the future, away! Away with the treasure of Pamela's lips! Pamela! He ran along the street, and now and then he jumped—the thrill of her!

Pamela! Pamela! And King Bozo! He now walked fast, her eyes, her soft, lovely, floating face, her darling voice, warning him, *Bozo*—his mind reeled, and alarm! had been in her *secret wish*—oh Pamela! Pamela! his heart cried, Me! Me!

# DREAM

THE ROAD left the highway and wound between farms and hills; a small wooden fence held the name of the school and the taxi went between fenceposts up a dirt road and stopped in front of a large screened in building. Thomas got out, he had arrived at college and was immediately confused in directions, he had seen the school lake to his right and also the dam; across the lake from the dam stood old and new buildings where classes were held.

He began along a dirt road, and at the top of a hill he crossed a bridge, and after asking directions he found the registrar's office; he announced and introduced himself and the next day, again going to the registrar's office, he walked along a dirt road and something was familiar although he couldn't find the hill and the bridge he began through a field of tall grass, he stood under tall trees darkly conscious of terror and fascination and beauty, density of air—he saw a fence; then he saw the dam. Later the registrar smiled; "You went the wrong way." Thomas laughed—

He sat on the edge of her bed drinking vodka and orange juice remembering walking along the highway at night with stars overhead following a downward slope through grass into a thicket, and emerging entered woods and came upon another road which he left, going up some wooden steps into a tavern where two or three farmers drank, standing—maybe knowing and not knowing or not remembering him, for they were different men, he had a drink by himself; they continued drinking, backs to him in the dark and wooden Klondike tavern lit by kerosene lamps—warm in a sense of home, of men and experience: déjà vu vanished walking down the highway he crossed over the shoulder and descended into woods, he was afraid it was dark and the earth was moist beneath him parting heavy leaves before him he moved slowly with rapid pulse, he stopped at the sound of running water; he got down on his hands and knees; he felt ahead of him, he was on a ledge and the ground cracked downward he tumbled in a panic, landing slightly bruised in a shallow brook; he got to his feet trembling and looked around there was nothing to see in utter darkness, he began slipping stumbling through water—into a mud wall, face colliding against mud, he put his hands on it, it rose above his head; he leaned his face and body against it, heart beating in a similar density of darkness.

He felt along the embankment, fingers gently touching touched concrete and moved back again to the mud embankment which sloped up; Thomas scrambled upwards—quickly hauling himself over the top and lying flat "on my stomach on the grass beside the dam over which water trickled; and across the night lake I saw lighted windows in old college buildings, where myself and unforgotten students worked," in Thomas's dream—drinking vodka and orange juice on the edge of her bed lonely for college, lonely for—the encounter—re-encounter—he reached for it—*reaching*


WHAM!

He stepped out of the cab and heard his name spoken. He closed the door and stepped to the sidewalk to encounter Billy and Vivian Earl coming down the street, going out for the evening again; he shook hands with Earl in a difficulty, Thomas had compulsively promised to telephone and hadn't, Earld seemed to understand, though, and he and Thomas slightly talked, Earl looked at Vivian waiting for her to direct; Thomas faced them a little between them although he was a few steps away, she doesn't like although she does, a little, my eccentricity in me makes her nervous, a smile is her personal humor, I from in me see you; face involving feminine pleasure of disdain; in the distance behind her eyes I am represented as though she faced me smiling goodbye, the expression in her eyes is gauze-like—subtle—yet incredibly saying hello; "We have to go; we don't want to be late," Vivian said; she took Earl's arm; they said goodbye and walked away. Thomas went home depressed and sat on the bed; his wife sat beside him and asked what was wrong. "I saw Earl and Vivian on the corner just now," Thomas said; "I'm nver sure how they really react to me—and I was pissed at coming home from a hard day's uselessness to see Earl and Vivian going out again." Thomas's wife smiled inwardly; she prompted him to look at his jealousy. "He needs people and places," she said, "and more than you he can go visiting;" Thomas said, "God they go to a movie a friend's house or the 5 Spot and hear Monk."

"He selects it," Thomas's wife said; "I don't seem to be able to do those things," Thomas said, and she said "Until you want to, he keeps himself in control so he can anytime," she said, and Thomas asked himself if he wanted to go to a movie (no) "Do you want to go to a movie?" he asked his wife, she shook her head and he asked himself if he wanted to visit someone, no, "Do you want to visit someone?" he asked her, "Who do we like?" she asked him; "I don't want to be a clam in society," Thomas said unhappily, and Fanta let him see him drifting along and dying. He agreed he could surely give himself away, yes you can, why I'd give me away before I'd take me, Fanta opened the door and Thomas remembered the dream conscious of a change in face, "I dreamed I was crossing the street to our left, but at the same time I was in Earl's loft looking out the window at a convertible, I approached our loft looking out our window at a convertible with red leather upholstery and a glittering chrome dashboard—radio, cigarette lighter and a brilliantly waiting steering wheel; do you remember we were in the bar the other night? And Earl came over with the news that Nathaniel was married?" Thomas's wife nodded. Thomas: "We invited him to join us but he said no, he said he had to go home, Vivian was expecting him, he had borrowed a car, he said, they were going to the beach early the next morning, and because he had to return the car that evening they wanted to get an early start. I was jealous of him because he had a car; because he could drive, but the car in my dream wasn't the car Earl was anxious to return, it was *my* car, powerfully primed and waiting for me to get in and go, but I couldn't drive it so well as Earl—"

"Why?"

Earl was a tall, quiet guy. He lived around the corner from my loft.

In the old dream I was young and old at the same time, peering between the slats of the manger watching Bill Earl and my wife. He lay in the straw on the floor of the barn, he was on his side looking down into my wife's face as she lay on her back yet a little awkwardly away from him with her head on his arm looking up at him; they were talking; my distress and disappointment with my wife turned into anger and agony and confusion and I went to them, I stood over them, Earl looked up at me carelessly and the cruel queen at his side was remote from me; there had been a time she had spent with me, but that was all gone, she was with him now; I had been deleted.

How could I be angry at Earl on a street corner as he and his wife were on their way to hear Monk or visit Nat's brother or have dinner with that trickster Jackson Hatfield? I was jealous—and I actually liked Earl, and Vivian, for it: it was the way they were *regardless*—of dreamy illuminatives like— me, Thomas a Crimmins meandering with Fanta, I'll—twenty years from now I'll see Earl and Vivian on their way to visit someone, no escaping it, and I'll still be jealous just as when Earl borrowed the car to go to the beach, but in my dream I parked the car in front of his loft, not mine, and when I looked out his window there it was. I fear the drive through the known—a whole geography I know awaits me, just as it keeps Earl and Vivian out for the evening, I saw them on the street —or, as I was coming home in the dream I cross the street to my loft looking out Earl's window at my car, or go to work in underground thunder and take the luxury of a cab home, and when I get out of the cab I see Earl and Vivian going out again, I say hello as I've said hello to them on the street before, or hello at the bar they are always just leaving 'only stopped in for a moment,' having been at Jackson's for dinner*—how

---

*Jackson hadn't been at college two weeks when I climbed in his bed giving him a big story to tell about my name and face in his large and small resentments, hate, envy, and lust.

The sexual guilt that had become the reaction, or, my reaction to my memory of the first weeks I knew Jackson seemed, ten years later, to

can they visit Jackson so often? His right hand fights his left and his feet trip each other—but he was a pretty thing he hadn't been in college two weeks when I climbed in bed after him, which now gives him a sneering story to tell about my face and name in large and small resentments hate and envy and lust I am the same face Jackson first saw, yet as I grow older, different figures, among them him move in and out of it

---

be usable in his mouth, and he talked, revealing his power to puzzle me with myself, as I refused to recognize my double sexual image. I thought there was only one image for me, like a pyramid with a large evil base and I dissolved into bed with Jackson—and men and women for a decade a certain notoriety for sexual festivity. My mind turned into an exploding star; sparks sizzled up my sides to the top of the pyramid; I was really something to see.

Thomas and his wife went to a party at his friend's apartment—the famous Negro writer's East 14th Street place, and saw Jackson there, drunk beside his wife on the sofa in front of the window; Thomas said hello to forward tilting Jackson, Jackson's lips were trembling and brimmed with saliva, and with a furious look at Thomas, Jackson tossed a half a glass of rye down his throat which came suddenly right back up and out in a stream back into the glass again; Jackson looked at it and choked; he set the glass on the table in front of him and gripping locked his hands together holding on, and looked up at Thomas. "You don't know it," Jackson said, "and in your star struck way I'm sure you don't care;" Thomas watched him swallow spit while he Jackson gathered powers Thomas had given him—Thomas's fear to own his sexual selves; Jackson took position in front of Thomas, Thomas smiled and stuttered hello; Jackson discarded the self Thomas wouldn't own—he waved it away—and leaned toward Thomas as if to lean into him, furious of Thomas's relation with himself, and others in Thomas's manner, and Jackson shook his head his eyes drilling into Thomas's, "no," he repeated, "though you are pretty, though you are bright, bright Crimmins, I think I even know why *you* don't know." Jackson separated from himself rising taking Thomas's arm leading Thomas into a corner holding his arm whispering informing Thomas that he Jackson had been up-as if it was a stage—a fiction in fact, and he who crawled across Jackson's sheets was one individual darting between other bodies coming so close it caused friction, the chills up my spine—one of me had moved me between the others, and as the players dashed dodging around between themselves battling for the possession of my mind (he was standing on a high platform in an old building in his home town in Missouri, and he, Thomas, looked over the edge afraid he was going to fall, and he fell stomach convulsing he falling seized one of

---

town—had spent two days and nights with a pretty girl who was in love with him. Thomas mentioned that was terrific, stammering he didn't understand why Jackson was telling him; of all people. Thomas's eyes were bright in his combination. But Jackson's eyes *glittered,* he tilted his head back and curled his lip he was now the wise avenger with the key to Thomas's past "You don't know," he whispered; and Jackson fondled his chin, but the one man knew so much he vanished becoming teenage twins and four eyes flashed as if Thomas had captured Johnny and Josie, yet as if bearing the burden of Jackson's history Thomas saw a figure behind the twins, or a figure of two figures, both left feet joined, trudging through The Hatfield Twins—who were shrinking—as through a dark and stormy night, children spat at them, and at Thomas, cussing him, and Thomas hesitatingly yelled, "I'm not yours you fucking goofy boatload of people, I—I'm MINE!"

And she came out of Jackson walking, she recognized Thomas and for a moment they were fascinated with each other; she was young and intuitive, her eyes twinkled and as though she winked at Thomas—that he pay attention to her—she told Jackson she had the feeling she met Thomas before—at college? Jackson's face changed, brightened, as she vanished laughing at her joke, but as Jackson believed anything she said the way she said it, he shouted—triumphant—"I knew about you FROM THE START!"

"HER!" Thomas angrily cried—he pointed into Jackson's astonished expression: "THAT'S your uptown girl!"

The one Thomas had gone for, naturally.

the light cords that hung from a checkerboard of hanging cords—chess strings—and hands clasped around the neck of one psyche, he gradually descended), turning me into (a machine in the sky) bed with Jackson, I reached what I reacted to in him, his boyish glamour, which forcefully pushing pulling drove me between me, to him; united with *self*—the general in the generalized first person—I'm coming to it! Listen! Listen! Progressions! Me, mine or mine-self my (own) self, mine my-self, my-self, myself mine *I* rushed through me to possess a fixity of face—Jackson features included—a thousand male and female features in a single splash of come, out of which springs I of time in face, me and mine a child a man a feminine goddess/destroyer and creator of my impulses and fiction in a car moving alongside my train—in Jackson's boyish face; he was very embarrassed. And, nothing.

When Thomas was fourteen he loved them; he followed them around after school, they were tall and they drove their cars fast; and in his loft in New York a man Thomas was on the trail of the living child within him.

"I loved them. They liked me well enough," he wrote, "and in a feminine way I felt they belonged to me—they delighted me and I envied their older ages, their size and their nights in their cars. One fellow was big; split tooth and a lisp; one fellow was short, he wisecracked and sharply dressed and the third fellow was nifty tightlipped fascination and I used to imitate the way he walked I could do it now; he could go down any world street." Thomas remembered his name, and wrote it down, *Airling*. Thomas's heart suddenly jumped! They called him—Thomas's writing hand shook as he stared at his written slip:

"A nifty tightlipped fascination and I used to imitate the way he walked I could do it now; he could go down any world street—" Robert Airling, but they called him—I gave him my love and awe at fourteen and at thirty two I give him my wife. No wonder. I am still there. I had written the following:

"A nifty tightlipped fascination . . . he could go down any world street. Robert *Earl*." Not *Airling*.

Thomas smiled in his wife's level eyes. "Still me."

She opened the taxi door and turned, smiled wanly, waved, got in. The cab lurched into the street and sped west across town.

"3C-28C," Thomas laughed, "speaks: attack the unknown." He asked Al,

"What do you think of her?" Al shrugged; Thomas said, "I saw a veil over her eyes, did you?" Al said "No," and his face clouded, irritated at Thomas's metaphorical nonsense. Then Al saw Thomas had seen him frown; Thomas smiled; then Al was glad Thomas saw him and felt grateful for Thomas's perception, for he loved Thomas because Thomas responded to him, but he reacted thusly apologising, "Well I just met her, maybe after I got to know her," "You would see," Thomas compulsively interrupted, "how guarded her eyes are."

Al was irritated by Thomas's lordly attitude, so, said, bitterly, "Of course." Thomas picked his nose and said, "I'm not attacking you; I'm after what it means. There isn't any veil, naturally, her eyes gaze out of her head like—" "Don't be childish," Al snapped, and began filling his pipe; Thomas said he hadn't finished, "but it seemed I saw a veil—right away— which partly explains why her face is so white, the color is behind her face—is her face a veil? That sleepy look—everything happens in—under? Behind? The outer face is fixed," he concluded; he complimented himself on the sentence, yet the alliteration sounded familiar as he had the feeling he was explaining his reaction to her to himself—as if Al was somebody else—and Al was! Thomas laughed; he tapped himself on the shoulder, "At it again? Convolution? What happened to *her?*" Thomas wiped his brow, sorry, sorry, don't want to scream on, etc., and he saw himself wanting to describe her, and he answered, "It interests me. What can you expect? I have no style to speak my interest, I have me to speak and there isn't any veil, except maybe in my eyes, but it's still what I see so it seems to reveal my creation of her, which is not her, but my vision *intrigues me,* I love it and can say—I'm *fascinated* by her, I love her in a way I don't understand—I ought to, too. I'm a fool." He looked at Al. Thomas's introspective eyes sharpened and his face became the words he was about to use—Al couldn't take his eyes away from Thomas's—struck by Thomas speaking, gesturing, and Al, realizing how intensely he felt about Thomas, missed what Thomas said; Thomas had come to a conclusion, Al had just caught the last few words he clenched his teeth searched back for the beginning of Thomas's sentence, but Thomas, though not speaking, was gesturing, and Al panicked because he didn't know what the gestures meant because he hadn't heard—etc., Al searched on, at the same time frightened of Thomas because Thomas would be disappointed with Al, and Al would almost rather die than disappoint him, suddenly Al saw Thomas get in a cab and go away, and self-conscious in Fanta's grip (Thomas's metaphor, Thomas again; Why can't the cocksucker-combination say fantasy like everybody else! Because he's a writer. Cocksucker—bad or good? Al's hands were trembling), and he had the feeling he was a whole audience between himself

and Thomas—a man rose from the crowd, and cried—strangely, "Let *him* know it!" A woman screamed "NO" and a different man jumped up and called to the first, *"You're* afraid to
know!" Al—feverishly—smoothed his face down working and
wondering why he wouldn't let himself remember what he had
heard Thomas say he set his eyes straight and fixed his lips
and opened his ears he nodded faking comprehension comprehending he had missed the boat—But—!—Thomas said it—
Thomas's right fist was in the air! His left hand pointed to
his raised right arm he shook his fist savagely, "—for her,"
he snarled through teeth; yet Thomas asked himself, "Which
one? Thomasina or the girl in the taxicab?"

He saw her face, lips parted and eyes closed in passion
against the back of his neck, his left arm behind her back
his right arm between her legs he bent and kissed her navel;
she kissed the back of his neck running her hands through
his hair—but the girl in the taxi was moving away, his fist
turned into a flat hand, he lit a cigarette smiling thinly as Al
was wondering where Thomas was; Al had caught up. "No,
no," Thomas said, and he shook his head translating to himself, to Al, *"If* she was mine. She isn't. She's hers, with a veil
over her inwardly guarded—" What! Secret, he whispered,
her secret vagina! Vagina? Woman! Woman! Thomas's lust
cried out, "Rip away the veil! Pull her out of her head and
deliver the hidden pussy to ME!" Al lit his pipe and grinned.

"She's got you." He puffed.

Thomas bent over laughing and clapped his hands. "She
does indeed."

He added, "All my life; even before I met her—" Al scowled,
"What the fuck does that—" Thomas cried out striking his
chest his balls his head and pointed to the sidewalk—"As I
walk down the *street!* and now that I see her I—say—I cry—

there THERE YOU ARE MY *darling!*" But Al underrated his intuition and world knowledge of stereotyped phrases— Al said, pointing the way the taxi had gone, *"She* isn't yours." Suddenly he added—with eyes in surprise and delight: "Or you!"

Thomas snapped his fingers angrily. "How damned right! Right, and right again! A double rightness, how God damned bitter it is, and I lean towards her! I try and bring her into my arms—try to bring that bitch Thomasina into my *arms,* but my arms are my arms, dearness I feel—Yie! Yie! Naked and darling—my darling! How I desire—how I yearn to possess you!"

"The other one went that way," Al pointed. "Your arms are all yours."

Thomas took his friend's hand saying, "She did, you're right, they are, she did," and stepped back casting his cigarette into the street, face flushed and eyes a little glazed; he pointed to his chest; he began to cry; he lowered his head tapping his finger against his chest repeating he didn't know how to own them, he had always given them to her, he whispered it was impossible; Al asked, oddly,

"Do you look like her?" and Thomas muttered, "Not in fact; only in face," and snapped his fingers again and looked up, he thrust his index finger in the air. "There is more to this than we—than I think—come in 3C dash 28C!" He grinned; he wiped his eyes, said goodbye to Al, and—stumbling took a few steps and turned, said goodbye again, winking, grinning, "Wow!" turned away, tripped and went home.

He heated the coffee, filled the cup, added sugar and cream, sat down lit a cigarette and conjured her pale face and figure before him, and seeing her he warmed, yet once he looked into her eyes he saw how fixed and troubled she was; and then her face was troubled, and looking at that face saw she was absent from it—lovely but not there; another figure was there—concealed within and perspiration appeared on Thomas's forehead; a continual searching into her eyes met the gaze of an inner woman who was as if asleep—as Dracula in the sunlit hours; the deadly eyes were half open, looking dully through the eyes in the face of flesh and he realized he must separate the girl in the taxi from Thomasina and from the inner figure he saw now, and as he studied her outer hair and dear body two things startled him—she actually did not want him—and not only did not want him, she had actually forced him out of her—head; Thomas felt a chill, remembering.

He remembered how she sat in the darkness of the far rear corner of his loft—the night she had come to supper, and after supper she had sat at his desk and made a whispered telephone call; Thomas left his wife at the table and nervously moving as in a trance into the darkness of the back of the loft—not knowing what he was doing, standing as a statue in the dark unconsciously listening to whispering—realized he was alone, the whispering had stopped, and from out of the dark silence a strange harsh hiss commanded *"Go. Away!"* which he did, yet leaning, bending backwards drawn to the voice of her sexual phantom, and that was the first. Through it came the second, like sound out of an engine, the drawings her aesthetic lover had done of her naked figure—now appearing, clinched it as Thomas remembered the darkly shaded charcoal flesh the artist had included in his attitude of his life within her, for he walked in her he walked in her, not her flesh, not terribly vital, her head without face was turned to a huge sweeping black wing, the tip of which now crossed her face as her body of flesh helplessly leaned beyond a spatial blackness at her feet; the aesthetic artist who had feared her identity had drawn the black wing of the raging creature in her outside her.

Thomas's perceptions came out of his experience and lined up within a dark voice from a far corner that had drawn him to it—why—why—seeing the great black wing cross her face in the drawing—the veil—she wanted him to leave, he left, yet he leaned towards it, her, her secret sexual configuration, he backwards leaned, he had heard, and desiring and looking he saw the hands and arms the bodies the writhing naked bodies of the creature and the whispering girl covering the telephone with her hand—go. Away—she waited until he had left—then! And then as he left leaning backward to her—pulled back by!—looking over his shoulder at her fixed and dimly white and weirdly featureless mask whispering in darkness "I'll be over soon, am leaving now" kissing and caressing the other, Thomas cried out, disillusioned, invisible—*not mine!* And he left—Thomasina pulling him back even as he moved towards his wife, Thomasina so hotly desiring to strike fire in—shadows, in space—in the pale white veil of face whispering to the girl on the other end of the line—now fiercely—a voice of scarcely controlled lust from the lips of the powerful Dracula within; utterly, wildly, awake.

Carol stood at the sink peeling zucchini; Al sat at the table nervously smoking his pipe, puffing, tamping, puffing, waiting for the knock on the door to signal the arrival of Carol's mom and dad from home—Carol was pregnant; Al rose and stepped to the sink beside her, put his hand on her rounded belly and kissed her ear, she drew away muttering his name saying "Don't"; he smiled—gazing upon her a cloud of fear crossed his heart convinced he would be a weak father; her mom and dad would come into the apartment where he feared and worried and watched his baby fill his wife in spite of his feelings.

Footsteps sounded on a flight below and Carol tensed, her hands moved up and down, and Al said her name, tenderly into her apprehension, she looked at him and smiled, her eyes filled with tears as double footsteps approached the flight below. Al went close to Carol and she put her head on his chest; Al was already seeing the father mother eyes searching his face and figure within the wooden railroad flat. A despair of poverty swept through him and the objects in their newly-wed daily existence sat raped without paint or neighbor, only the rocker had a rug in front of it and Carol's hairbrush lay on the barren dresser with no mirror; their legal match of hearts, with Carol pregnant now, formed the only union they knew in Salvation Army furniture on the top wooden floor in the sky above Chinatown; Al filled his pipe and went into the front room and sat in the rocker puffing and talking to his nervousness as four feet shuffled up the stairs, he clenched his teeth and fists and went into the kitchen, heart pounding; Carol had turned and wiped her hands, taken off her apron

and was facing the door and the knock, together Al and Carol
went, ushering in mom and dad with hellos handshakes and
embraces.

The outcrying world of mother and father swept through
and filled the flat; they stood and talked and sat talking and
wanting to know, scrutinizing Al. And Carol's father sitting
across the table from Al. And Carol rather shyly asked what
it was *he* was eating—invisibly reaching his hand across the
table, eyes blazing, holding his daughter in an iron embrace—
mother made a tentative stand of affection beside Al in her
habit of thwarting her husband smiling and snarling at and
to him, squash, Carol said, zucchini, Italian squash watching
her father inwardly snarling, smile all over his face: to Al
"Writer, eh?" Al nodded, and Carol's father mentioned he,
at one time, and the favorite was Chekhov and Al nodded, Chekhov, Chekhov was certainly, very good and after lunch, over
coffee Carol's father asked Al what he did to make a living
rubbing his thumb over his first two fingers grinning and
humming, "You've got to have money." Al was a trucker's
helper moving furniture and her father smiled and sneered
nodding and Carol's face darkened, Al looked at her father's
calloused hands by the coffee cup around Carol's body with a
hot glitter of hate and time-revenge in his eyes; he's a long
way from Carol's mother, Al saw, and the man and woman
sat beside each other to give Carol the best life they could,
withdrawing into themselves with her, Al saw that the man
profoundly hardly cared about him, Al, and—Al was frightened. "I'm looking for a full time job," he lied, stammering
there was an agency a good agency good meaning sympathetic
to creative people—"I made a cake!" cried Carol, rising her
father lightning-like beside her as Al rose shoving his chair
back "It's all right, Daddy," she said over her shoulder, taking

the cake from under the plastic dome; she put it on the table and cut it while Al got the saucers Carol's mother put the coffeepot on the table and Carol served cake, Al got cream and sugar and they ate cake and drank coffee; "Tell us about the ceremony!" Al and Carol burst into hysteria which they (almost tearfully) suppressed remembering Herman Katz at City Hall, the honeymoon night, a Spanish restaurant a movie and a bottle of wine at home her father's invisible hands gripping Carol's shoulders said, what they should do, if they wanted a *real honeymoon*, would be to visit *them* at home for a couple of weeks and Al and Carol brightened anything to leave the city going dark in memory of possessive oppressive rooms of home; Al glanced at Carol's doubt and their eyes met, they said they would definitely visit, but not just yet, the baby and coffee and cake as Al's mother and father appeared in Carol's father's concern—Al said he hadn't told—his folks yet and Carol's father's face assumed surprise, bewilderment, a shared sorrow; misunderstanding and a vindictive triumph and a curiosity as it darkened and made Al nervous, he said he had problems he had to first solve, "What kind of problems?" her father asked, "You can't even tell your mother you're married? That your—what & why, father would be— what, because—" Al said he didn't know how to explain what he meant and Carol's father said if Al was a writer, shouldn't he—Al answered it was part of the reason, if there was a reason, why he was a writer to enter those problems—and he said he wanted to tell his mother and father but—first—he must first, tell himself, Carol's father's face clouded and opened downward in an exclamation "If you're married you're married!" and he invisibly sat beside his daughter in proof, and, arm around her waist said "See?" Al said it wasn't— yet—altogether—"It takes years for a marriage to become real as a marriage otherwise it's two people across the room from each other—separated—when you're *married* you can't tell yourself from the marriage," and Carol's father heatedly said Carol's baby was real, and as Al shook his head how was Al going to accept that—and when? in ten—? "You'd better get a grip on yourself," Carol's mother agreed with arms around herself as Al agreed yet explaining they had been married a week and Carol's father said *evidently* they had been with each other longer than, Al nodded with Carol's mother saying yes, but being married was different than not being married, Carol's father said, true and asked Al what he was going to do for money, money was necessary, he had worked all his life and raised his children and he pointed at Carol he pointed at her sister he pointed at her brother in a line across the nation behind her slightly slapping Carol— independently leaving him mentioning Daddy had helped her brother's family her sister's family—showing they too lived independent and not independent still leaned to him like a secret darkness her father conjured before Carol threatening her in his need to turn from—*no face*—opened his hands, he had worked hard; he had made sacrifices; he said he had raised his children and witnessed two weddings; but he missed this one; yet he *only* wanted to be sure Carol was secure in, Al agreed interrupting breaking the spell—yet the spell was cast, Carol was dazzled by her father's need, for Carol was the baby Al had taken away, and as Carol's mother smoothed the waves violence threw between them Al wondered how many years it would take for the man to realize Carol was out of his hands into Al's hands—on Al's side of the table beside Carol—possibly never, or almost, yet if her father did—not a day to look forward to for the man might then react, and out of the turmoil of violence Al lent to her father in that future possibility Al flashed that more lives were there than four, more than the fifth of Carol's baby, more than the sixth and seventh of her brother and sister, the eighth and ninth of their wives and the numbers of their children; there were lives in Carol's father's past that had never been lived, that stayed darkly in the distance down the undergrowth in the tunnel of her father's restless and avoided accumulated experience—did Carol represent any of those lives? The question seemed to strike true; and from out of the man's past lives rose and swarmed against the faceless glass of Al's and Carol's future—and with finality the future of her father, Al had a bitter fantasy Dear Mom & Dad I know you don't care, I'm married my wife is expecting a baby and both of us understand we are living within my wife's father's unacknowledged past, my wife holds hands with her father before me and her father rejected me long ago, and the feelings that pass between the four of us here set sirens screaming—I siren—Al put his head in his hands. Carol's mother and father stared, "Al," Carol said. Al, to himself: All these feelings would turn us woefully away from the dream—as if we fight to blind ourselves from the dream Carol's father rejected in his youth, form of perception, intuition and true emotion. For three days they went sight seeing around the city, and said goodbye in Grand Central; as they talked on the platform, Carol's father seemed to separate from what he had been, he told Al to write—"your mother and father, your mother should know." "I will," Al said, and the two men met differently in a handshake of farewell, the thaw of a three day freeze; Carol's father's soft accent had fallen on "mother"—"your mother should know"—revealing Carol's stories of the closeness of her father with his mother, warmth and affection, attention and trust; Al was touched. Carol's father turned, and, taking Carol's hand put it between his calloused fingers looking into her eyes, and though his face was averted from Al, Al saw what came into Carol's face and he shuddered, knowing the spell was being cast again, and the inner eyes of the old father blazed, drawing Carol away from Al—away from the world—and when her father, holding her eyes with his—softly spoke that she be a good girl, Carol's eyes lowered demurely, she smiled, nodding, and the unconscious genius the old savage king swelled and thumped his chest—his maiden daughter turned, and glanced contempt at Al: Al: stunned, and double-crossed, fell reeling across the platform in Carol's promise of a visit, home, they'd be home the first week next month.

# MAGNETIC NORTH

*for Bob*

JUST INSIDE the open doors to the bar, where he stood, the salesman saw a little sunny place. He looked through it at the street. He smiled, feeling solitude which remained unbroken as a fellow came through the doorway and went into a phone booth and made a call leaving the door open. He drew no response and hung up, coming out of the phone booth and standing near the salesman at the bar. He ordered a beer. The bartender, dim and bulky, drew the beer.

The fellow drank, wiped his brow, said "Hot."

The salesman nodded, noting twinkling eyes, said "And humid."

"It is humid," the fellow said. "This darned city."

They struck up a conversation, and though the fellow seemed uncomplicated there were complicated reasons why, the salesman believed what the fellow said yet he wondered at the smoothness; they talked for a while, each about the past, the fellow had been in the Second World War and also in Korea. He had been in "a long time," and the salesman wondered if anyone anywhere in the world would be affected by the presence of this ex-soldier who seemed to merge near with far; the salesman felt his inner ear tune in to the unspoken ex-soldier, to sift and weigh the innuendoes for precise meanings, and his hearing was like the surface tension of water which held the needle of knowing poised, to gradually but conclusively swing to magnetic north, the difficult male complex under the face.

The salesman heard what he almost heard, saw what he

thought he saw: a handsome fellow divided in desire, distrust and fear of himself, and fear of other men, yet moving toward other men, to circulate in the dangerous but necessary air of and for other men's response, other men's response frightened, constricted and seemed to unite powerful directional forces which used the constricted ex-soldier to their end, sent him to other men with a subtly feminine friendly and topical manner, a glass of beer and a sensation all's well with the world.

A handsome fellow, a stylish fellow with sandy hair and freckles and twinkling eyes, a youthful winning smile, he was no youth. And through the friendly expression, behind the smile lines at the eyes friction was at work, doubt and fear and a miserable guilt, and far away in the eyes an unbearable self-consciousness, the ex-soldier was rarely where he visibly was, mind hardly knowing what it did know, and the ready smile and friendly manner at once complicated the complex and froze his reaction to himself.

He liked the company of men, but he was confidently influenced by a nagging hag inside him to be the companion to other men on their terms a friendly drink and a sensation all's well with the world, a little uncertain though, guilty he, he wanted to absorb the ways other men were instead of his ways, the ways they saw and felt and reacted which he was afraid to do, afraid in front of them they might react, so he got easy going, they made him secretly guilty and self-conscious (he secretly saw himself looking all the time at women telling himself "look at you looking at her"), and his hag sent Sandy to other men he needed who might spoil what he saw of himself, so in that way he got as close to other men as he could, wanting to come to an understanding with the secret which made them perceptive, get close with what he wouldn't get probably couldn't, it was too late for himself he was sure, she sneered.

Who was this nervous salesman? The ex-soldier felt a friction-like chill and became generous. A little condescending. Curious.

"Would you have a beer with me?"

DREAM:

WANTING TO fuck Harriet, but she wouldn't let me unless I did something about a contraceptive as she—didn't have her diaphragm with her, at a party? In a living well (slip) room—brightly lit; I agree to do something; she is away and I am also away. She is waiting for me, lying on a bed and I am in a room, I have her body—no head no arms or legs but as if legs, for there is an interference with my hands trying to get the string in. A long string hurriedly but poorly wound around itself, saturated, slippery with vaginal jelly—first I pushed bits of rags in her, as deep as I could, and then the string, yet as I pushed the string which kept slipping, the rags were only pushed out, and I worked feverishly, but as I pushed the rags in again the string came out, and my hands got in each other's way, I pushed the string the rags came out—I was talking with Elsene on the telephone, telling her something. She was busy at home, and wasn't concerned with me in the way I wanted her to be, her attention was elsewhere. I talked rapidly, trying to convince her I was in trouble in lust, but she was preoccupied—listening as hard as she could she couldn't get it, and I heard her voice, and she was really on the other end of the line, for while I was talking with her on the telephone I was yet with her, for I saw her, sitting in a chair, her mind on other things talking to me, but my presence was beside her— I held the telephone in my hand and heard her far apology— she'd call later, couldn't talk now, sorry, but the kids—she hung up, I had a brief sense of the boy and the girl by a kind of window complex, facing the very bright light of sun, but they were in trouble and she rising, rushed to them.

# THE MOVING MEN

I SEE HIM standing beside his battered station wagon his eyes
peer out from the pale cliff of his beard he is smiling in his
red beard in my mind where he stands for me to see the rest
of my days: kind and lonely in the absence of himself as age
without childhood he is apart from his face and existence
within a glance and his ear or wrist resembles the tilt of the
car in distance with the road wooden buildings shattered glass
of the tailgate window.

I remember Charles' personal touch to air in him, Charles
reached into the miles and miles of pale ghost landscape standing beside that station wagon full of books magazines newspapers pamphlets scraps of and torn notebooks the first few
pages of each underlined w/marginal notes in an unreadable
handwriting old shoes old underpants in dust old station wagon
old man in time without age, old highway man young student
pointing with the stem of his pipe face up as he makes his
point to Charles' teaching response.

Years later I saw him in the Cedars he was driving through
to D.C. he said, he parked the station wagon outside the bar
he was glad to see me we shook hands he glanced into my
memory where he stood, student behind the red beard he
glanced sadly away how is Charles? I hold him of Charles
writing in Gloucester and he nodded, good, as his slanting
visible and invisible existence made its strange slow tumble
forward remembering Charles and school, remembering the
appearance of Charles into him remembering the sound of
Charles at college, intuition of Charles at college, his life in

mornings on the porch at college overlooking the lake with Charles going down his highway remembering as the road dipped and slanted into distant towns and pages shadows hills and mountains hints and lakes and threads and intersections clues and ends of nerves which Charles took and sewed and tied together making the construction as they moved.

# A LETTER TO PHILIP GUSTON

I HAVE A watercolor, Bill Cushner said, and he held his hands up and began putting the scene together in air, over here his right hand settled in front of him are the contours of fields, and over here his left hand waved is a road and there are trees, there is a character in oddly colored clothes on the road here, he said, and beyond is the sea.

Yet over here his right finger circled there is a color and his face changed as he said: a—he paused, there is a color there, in the field that takes my eye away. He looked at me, his eyes are gray and black and blue. Every time I looked at it I went from here to here his left hand swerved, and I, each time I, I finally took it to the right *and* left, I had it retouched so I could see it, the color I mean was a little faded, d'ya see? he asked. Even there it was just there, it was as if it was also there, and I grinned and told him how you reacted when I mentioned my interest and curiosity in that green—in the green in the lower right hand part of the one at Sidney's, in fact the day after your opening, and you yelled Let me alone about the fucking GREEN, and I also thought about Rothko, sizing the whole thing yellow—first, then starting and I remembered my own dismay at changing a painting towards the red on the left and in the end beginning all over again, after all the tough work, still the painter's problem the color calls the painting. that funny color on the right, it is a watercolor and he probably put it aside beginning a new one starting with that problem color, I would, I did, looking and looking at that color wondering where it was going knowing something was next to it, something invisible—or not there—was beside it, and away from it a little to the left and something slanted down to the right, what—as in anxiety of can you hear me? Unh huh, what color was it. Well, I went to it, and stood outside it looking at it, and I was within it, looking at it and painting it, and years later thought of you when I saw it again in the watercolor he described—this here, that there—I mean seeing you in there was great, as he talked about that color in that field.

SHE CROSSED the crowded tavern and sat next to him at the table. He was drunk. "Hello," she said. "Remember me?"

He looked at her.

"I went to New York again," she said, "you weren't at your old address so I asked around. Somebody in that bar told me you had come to Provincetown, so I thought I'd come up to Provincetown!"

"That's swell," he said. "How have you been?"

"Well, that's a big question, if you mean it seriously, but you don't mean it seriously. You hardly mean it at all, and not even nicely." She looked at him. He was older now, a little gray. "I want to tell you something," she said.

He looked at her; she smiled. "I was in Saint Louis this spring, and I saw your old psychoanalyst Doctor Sommer at a party, and as we know each other *fairly* well, I asked him if he remembered you. He said yes and asked how you were and what you were doing, is it fifteen years? I told you you were writing, and he was very pleased. He said—"

But the look on his face frightened her. "Don't you want to hear what he said? Still the same!" she sang. "You haven't changed at ALL!"

## OF THE DREAM

THE LIVING ROOM of this house is not coldly modern, it has a sense of warmth, a touch of impulsive indulgence, and character; newspapers are scattered over arms of chairs, ashtrays are full, magazines and comic books are helter skelter as if suddenly thrown down, and there are cups and glasses half full of coffee, and milk. As if they suddenly decided to take in a movie or visit someone. The room is softly lit.

The kitchen beyond is brightly lit, and cluttered.

A glass door with aluminum trim, leading from the living room to the back yard, is a shadow; the time is twilight.

The front door opens slowly, and a man enters wearing a dark blue suit and a white shirt open at the collar, black socks and black shoes. He closes the door quietly and comes into the living room. He is rather hesitant, and stands in the center looking the room over. He begins to move to the glass door, but stops, and without dramatic effect sits cross legged on the floor. There is a hardly audible sound, then, and then a murmuring sound, yet quite clear: of delighted children, which stops.

His face expresses concern. Yet though he is a serious man, his face shows curiosity and humor. It is a fact, a man's finite mask.

The glass door to the yard opens and a boy of about eight years enters and slowly closes the door. He stands watching the man. The boy is naked except for baggy underpants.

They look at each other, and without moving his eyes the

boy advances to the man, stopping within arm's reach.

Muted sound of delighted children. Stop.

The boy begins to silently speak, moving his lips without sound he is talking of everyday things, and gesturing his eyes are now turned inward, in his preoccupation of telling what has happened; the man puts his hand on the boy's hip tenderly; the man lowers the boy's baggy underpants and takes the boy's penis in one hand, and smiles; the boy continues his silent narrative gesturing freely, hands wandering before the man's face, the man, using his free hand, takes one of the boy's hands, and kisses it. The boy moves his hand away in a continuity of mime, and walks across the floor in a circle gesturing and speaking in a moving rhythm, and halts in a shadow, and turning warmly gazes at the man.

The man makes an amused slightly tightlipped smile, and holds his hands out before him, beckoning, and gently, yet with strength, questions,

"Where have you been?"

The boy crosses the room, and before he goes into the man's arms, he meets the man's eyes with his own, and gravely answers,

"I have always been you."

They embrace warmly, and the man whispers, emotionally, "At last."

# STRAIGHT LINES

*for Louie*

JACKSON FROZE in his tracks as firing broke out. A mortar exploded deep in the bushes behind him, and he ran deeper into the jungle veering to his right where Sergeant Lewis was with the other guys, and that turned out to be right. They didn't find the V.C. and the helicopter picked them up before nightfall; that night Jackson was drunk and doing the Monkey with the whores in Saigon. She was getting used to these compulsive Americans with trembling hands. He was nineteen years old, and when he finished the beer he drank the whiskey and started on the next bottle of beer, gazing at the four angry Negro paratroopers at the bar.

"Why drink so quick?"

He muttered, "Why not."

The air was tense.

Sunday morning Jackson got hit walking down a jungle road with Jacobs and Nicholson.

A poem! The V.C. did a dance! There was terrific gunfire. He went to his left fast, feeling nothing but terror. He collapsed on his knees near the trees hearing Jacobs yell that Jackson was hit. Jackson looked up at the sky, and then dared to look at the shattered bone in the hole in his shoulder. He passed out.

Woke in whiteness remembering the last lines of the poem, and hearing a roar of engines.

"You're going home, Private Jackson."

"Home?"

The poem, and the V.C. doing the dance by the jungle. Three

months and ten days to get to this. How about the others?

"My buddies!"

He felt his body rise, in sheer emotion for the living and dying; then he slept.

Mother and Dad were shocked at his bitterness. He had a hard time talking. He was in the backyard watching the squirrels in the trees, listening to gunfire, remembering the poem.

> *"Drive, fast kisses*
> *no need to see*
> *hand or eyelashes*
> *a mouth at her ear*
> *trees or leaves*
> *night or the days."*

Who had written it? Nobody knew. And the one guy who would was away at school, but lucky enough, in November Jackson got a letter from him. Joe had quit school and was painting in New York. He wrote saying he heard Jackson had been wounded.

"Why don't you come to New York? I can put you up."

Jackson went, and they had some good times, but Joe didn't know who wrote the poem. It sounded a little like—Sappho? No? Jackson told Joe about what happened, and about the V.C. doing the dance and Joe said a funny thing. He said he had written Johnson about it; he ought to talk with the V.C.

Joe was drunk and angry and Jackson was depressed; his shoulder hurt.

A couple of weeks later Joe invited a guy over, a skinny 4F character with acne that stammered it sounded like Zukofsky. But how do you talk to Zukofsky? You call him up. The next morning Jackson looked in the phonebook and there it was.

They met in the poet's apartment, and the poet asked Jackson to tell him exactly what happened; Jackson did, and the poet couldn't figure out how, or why, Jackson had heard his poem.

Around a year later Jackson wrote the poet this letter:

Dear Mr. Zukofsky,

Yesterday morning I remembered something; once, when I was a little boy, we were going on a trip. My father was driving, and at one point he began to drive faster, and then he kissed my mother, then he kissed the top of my head and messed my hair as we approached an intersection, I saw a truck abruptly swing out in front of us, right *there*, my father swerved our car, there was no accident, but as the truck had so quickly been placed, as if put there, I sort of *heard* "trees or leaves/night or the days" but I don't think it's your poem I heard, Mister Zukofsky, I think it was an a priori perception of death, deadly stillness, and I hope you aren't angry, I like the poem you wrote, but it's mine too. (I forgot to tell you I heard it before I was shot. Not after. Like the truck in a way, dead ahead and we were racing towards it.)

It was like this:

I went down the road with Jacobs and Nicholson, the jungle on both sides of us, in Viet Nam, and a V.C. stepped right out of the jungle with a tommygun, and was going to let us have it, fast, but Nicholson and Jacobs nailed him faster, and for one lightning instant his weapon was pointed at me, and as he started to spin he fired. It happened so fast, you can't believe it until you experience it. He came out of the jungle like a shadow, and he wasn't fifteen feet away, and when he was shot and began to spin, his gun swung to me and I saw he was going to fire, I heard—"Drive, fast"—then he fired.

# THE MAJOR CIRCLE

WHEN HE got back to Philadelphia—Chestnut Hill—boy were they glad to see him! Mom's open arms, her flowers, and her speeches and Dad with tears in his eyes. His buddies cheered and shed a few tears themselves.

He was a little thin but no wonder. So the idea was to give him good food and let him rest. What he needed was food and rest, he said they treated him okay but his eyes had a glaze of vulnerability, and Mom said after a few weeks at home he would, but he didn't, he wasn't. Toward Thanksgiving nobody could figure it out. He wouldn't talk.

The story was his plane had been hit and he had bailed out over V.C. territory, and had been captured, held prisoner for a few months, and in an undercover exchange, had been freed and after a lengthy interrogation, sent home.

I knew him in high school; I used to dream about him, then. He was a great ballplayer, and even though I was his age I used to chase his home runs and bring the ball back to him. In my dreams I stood at the foot of his bed, and he—the body essence I knew from the locker room—slept before my eyes. I would have been his slave; he was so beautiful. And shy. His hair was soft, so black it glinted blue. Skin just the lightest olive, and his amused or serious eyes sparkled innocence in darkness. His lips were dearly sensitive and when he flashed his grin and tilted his head I used to laugh out loud. I used to follow him down the street and read Saroyan to him. One night at a dance I told him it was the point of life to love. His eyes were contemptuous, and he manipulated me with a smile; "What's love, Dawson?" Well.

His highschool girl got him, and married him. She had chased after him, down hallways and streets from the Seventh Grade on, and hand in hand she went along with him after football games and summer dances, and after his second year at the University of Missouri he went into the Air Force, she always waiting at home. Then he went to Viet Nam. My mother wrote me when I was in Mexico about him being a carrier based jet pilot. He was a Major.

I came home and got an apartment in town, and continued writing. We never saw his name in the Philadelphia papers, but then we never really looked—the old gang was too preoccupied with wife and kids and money to really wonder anymore, and as they didn't come around, whatever interest there might have been faded away, and for a long time I didn't have my gang to drink with.

But when he was shot down it was in the papers; it was reported the Viet Cong had kept him in Convolution, he had been treated all right, etc., no war's over till people stop talking, and I got curious. (I saw him a couple of times. It was all he could do to say hello.)

In the following months I did some traveling, asking questions and adding things up, like a detective, until I saw it, and to make a long story short the Major had gone before this Viet Cong officer in a tent, and apparently the guy, the V.C. officer, like me, was pleasant enough, and the Major understood he, the Major, had been desired to be brought in alive, unharmed, and though exhausted and apprehensive, the Major responded with that Geneva Convention name rank and serial number stuff. The officer smiled. He said they knew that, and he asked the Major about his wife and kids; the Major said his name rank and serial number, and the enemy officer looked at him, and gravely:

"It is a dark and stormy night, the men are outside sitting around the fire," he said. He asked the Major about Mom and Dad and Philadelphia and childhood:

"Major! Tell us a story!"

Name, rank and serial number. The officer leaned forward and said persuasively,

"Tell us a story, Major."

Oh the arms and breasts of Chestnut Hill! *It was a dark.* Her Flowers! *And.* Her warm voice speaking that *endless magic. Stormy night.*

"Tell us a story, Major!" cried the enemy.

The Major began his story.

# MIRROR ROAD

I CAN SEE him still, across the room from me sitting on an upholstered ottoman in her living room, the mixed vodka drink in his hand, and in his world brain the Kiplinger Report. I see his open collar and short sleeves, his mid-western slacks and socks that match in contrast to his loafers. He is smiling and talking and his eyes are clear they are always clear, I remember his hands holding the drink, he holds himself in place, he was any place now or then with the drink in his hands holding tomorrow and thinking and going to see her and talking and smiling in the kitchen while she made the drink on the table inside the kitchen window which overlooked the worn driveway that ran out to Highway 66.

I saw him once as I turned the corner, he was in her driveway in shirtsleeves, he waved to me.

His oval face and thinning brown hair, and his perpetually clear eyes, his intelligent look and open collar and normal figure seemed hardly without secret—I or the panicky girl in me was afraid of him and he would frighten me or the girl-boy now as I know I see him in my mind as I know I am still able to draw myself to the darkness in my configurational fantasy of his violence, his face in dark rage would freeze me, I was younger then, and I shouted at him, we had been drinking all evening and into the night, it was late and I, bleary eyed and furious almost in tears from no response and the next day's memory of a one sided persistent and irrational scream to a pithy gray or white phallus without evil: I bounced: off his irrelevant question,

"Could I have another?"

Her rising to make him a drink, her returning with the drink, her returning to her chair and sitting down, I me in my, he in his, yet he appeared, he appeared and appeared without repeating, he appeared, his nose the quality of what's his name's nose, lips like those of that guy in A Kiss Before, his eyes like Colonel—appeared appeared without reappearing he became his face again and again an eye and ear a cliff, his hands around the drink, the vacant lot next door I lived around the corner and last spring towards end of evening my wife and I went around the corner the house was for sale and the yard was full of weeds and junk, I know the lighted windows and slanting frame and I see darkness and little things lost never found, lonely midwest woman, moving toward sixty she had never—with him never she said, away in my or her mind or in Southern Missouri with her daughter and son-in-law the cheerful and deductive absent minded unsure frightened woman fearing things at hand slip away the cigarettes were right there what happened to the tonic oh here, I wanted her to need my influences: I couldn't influence me and if I knew my answers I could help myself to her, me, I needed her to find more problems, answers were my joke: if I could offer sexuality to him for his response to me I'd have her with a larger package of me: more, I drank her endless supply of vodka and usually returned the next day for more to aid my trembling hands he rose to meet me, she said my name, and his, we shook, she said I was hung over, I laughed, he laughed, he was a man of her age, she made the drinks, I sipped mine, the sun came through the windows into the room where three world people talked and drank reality in the shape of themselves and I spoke to his appearing face, I had failed to reach myself I was self-conscious as I am when I am defensive about my obvious failure to reach myself in the presence of others, I gave in fell away he would step across the room and raise his fist, me-pussy said things to anger him and the eyes in his face appeared above his nose his chin his shirt buttons his hands and looked at me understanding how he felt about himself without showing what it was, again and again, repeat: he looked at me understanding how he felt about himself without showing what it was, he nodded and agreed and frowned and thought and laughed and rose to leave it was two in the morning, she was tired, I was drunk, he went out the door, I apologized, he said he would see me again we would talk some more, I flushed with resentment and was happy he wasn't angry, I asked her for two beers and stumbled home and drank them in my back yard and vanished into the next appearing sun changing and shifting from side to side to fool my need for the influential and inherent sense of mother and dead father which I hadn't let myself experience but thought I saw in other men and women, to know the male self without myself I would seize a man or me the way I would fear him as I appeared and appeared weary and frantic and frightened from my appearing face *what are you, I want to know what you are, I have no sense of what is in the face I see before me.* I washed my hands in the men's room where I work, I glanced up and saw a handsome man's face, the fellow saw me, his face was newly lined and in existence, his eyes saw mine and changed in perception—I then understood how far I was from my simple common mirrored face, lonely years and years from what I am.

# THUNDER ROAD

*In Memory of Ted Thornton*

IT WAS about 1 a.m. and raining hard. I heard a truck pull onto the gravel beyond the pumps. People got out, covered their heads with their coats and came inside, shook themselves and walked up to the counter: the man thin in rumpled suit, the girl about sixteen the boy about twelve they sat down and looked at me, the man had deep sockets and dark eyes flanking a sharp line down the middle of his face, he turned down his collar and I saw he was a man of God, they were pale and they were tired, the boy was exhausted the man looked at me and smiled, I smiled and he said two coffees and a hot cocoa, I made it and served it to them and watched them. They had been driving a long time, they were moving among them, in between where they started from and where they were going, they were distant and tired over coffee and cocoa, the boy bending over his cocoa lost in exhaustion and staring at the counter; the coffee revived the girl and she talked to the man, and she and the coffee revived him, he had two pairs of smiles and grins, fast and slow, his face changed when he smiled slow and when he flashed a grin nothing moved but his lips.

The girl had her hair pulled back under a bandana, she was plain but pretty and then I saw the boy was her brother in the way they talked—they didn't look much alike—then they were up, some money was on the counter, I saw the boy pull his collar over his head, the doors banged shut, tires ground on gravel and the truck headed down the highway, a wind moved the doors and the place was quiet; I fixed my hair and stood at the counter looking at the door like I was a statue in their three figures, now down the highway in the rain in my night, it thundered, and a gust of rain swung the sign above the parking lot.